THE AFFAIR OF THE JADE MONKEY

THE AFFAIR OF THE
JADE
MONKEY

by

CLIFFORD KNIGHT

DODD, MEAD & COMPANY
NEW YORK   1943

PRINTED IN THE UNITED STATES OF AMERICA
BY THE VAIL-BALLOU PRESS, INC., BINGHAMTON, N. Y.

TO

THOSE INTERESTING, HARD-WORKING MEN OF

THE NATIONAL PARK SERVICE,

WHO HAVE DONE

SO MUCH TO MAKE YOSEMITE NATIONAL PARK

THE MOST POPULAR OF OUR

COUNTRY'S PLAYGROUNDS.

I

ALTHOUGH it was mid July, patches of snow still gleamed on the high peaks of the Sierras. Shadows in deep valleys and on mountain meadows not yet reached by the morning sun were like somber velvet, and the heavily forested area of Yosemite National Park stretched eastward as a great dark sea rolling up to break in white foam in the crest of the range.

Jerry Straker had washed up his breakfast dishes and hung his dish cloth and tea towel on the line to dry. There were fresh deer tracks in the dusty soil underneath the clothesline. He had heard sounds of deer in the gray dawn. A porcupine had been at work again in a near-by tree, if freshly peeled bark meant anything to his experienced eye.

Straker climbed back up the steep wooden stairs to his glass-enclosed quarters in the fire lookout, thinking as he'd often thought before that the only difference between where he lived and a goldfish bowl was that on Trumbull Peak few came to observe him in his high, conspicuous privacy. The men of the Park Service didn't count; they were fellow employes and, like the deer and porcupine and occasional bear, a part of the landscape. He meant the outsiders.

A small haze of dust drifting up from the dirt road that wound through the second growth pine to the flattened mountain top caught his attention and he wondered who was coming up so early in the day. The week before there had been a Los Angeles newspaperman and his wife, who with another couple, were riding around in the superintendent's open car. They'd come up from the near-by Yosemite Valley floor piloted by the park forester just to look around, and maybe write something either for a paper or to put in a book. He didn't remember which. Their names were in the visitors' register over on the broad west window ledge.

There was no sign of smoke anywhere this morning, but the ground cover was drying out on the slopes and the humidity was low. Good weather for a forest fire. He looked westward to where he could see the dim outline of Mt. Diablo near San Francisco, almost a hundred and fifty miles away; the summer haze already was rising and would soon obscure it. The day would be hot again down in the big valleys.

The approaching car whirled around the final turn in the road and drew up underneath the lookout. The tall, spare figure of Floyd Plummer got out, followed by a stranger. Straker wondered what the chief ranger of Yosemite could want. As he looked down upon them the pair turned toward the wooden stairs of the lookout.

"Morning, Jerry," Plummer called up.

"You're out early, Floyd. Must have started before breakfast."

The chief ranger laughed and the two began to climb. They clumped up the final steps and entered the square, glass-sided room.

"Jerry, I want to introduce you to Professor Rogers— Jerry Straker, old Alaska sourdough turned fire lookout."

"You've got an airy perch up here, Mr. Straker," said Huntoon Rogers, as the two shook hands. "No end of view."

"None at all."

The fire lookout's gray eyes shielded by habitually narrowed lids thoughtfully inspected the younger man who confronted him. He was tall and broad shouldered; his eyes were a mild blue and his nose was strong. He wondered what sort of professor he was; he seemed a friendly fellow, though.

"I suppose you need a good pair of eyes in a place like this."

"I've got 'em, Professor. Always did have good eyes." Jerry Straker picked up the scuffed pair of ten-power binoculars and gave them to Rogers. "Have a look around."

Rogers adjusted them to his eyes after a moment's sweep over the wide expanse of forest and mountain, and gazed through them.

"They're too powerful for me. I don't get much out of them." He gave them back to Straker. "You don't have to cover this whole area, of course? I mean there are other fire lookouts in Yosemite?"

"Oh, sure. Come here a minute." He led the way just outside the door to where the stairs ended in a narrow railed landing. "Now, north of here just this side of the Tuolumne grove of big trees, there's a lookout," he explained, raising his arm to point out the spot. "Then still farther—away over there on North Mountain where he can look over into the Hetch Hetchy area there's another lookout. By the way, do you see a white house in there on the shoulder of the mountain? It wouldn't be more than just a dot of white if you can see it at all."

Rogers strained his eyes in the direction Straker indicated.

"No, I don't," he said after several moments.

"I don't either. There isn't any there."

Chief Ranger Plummer laughed and Rogers looked puzzled. Straker went back inside and Rogers followed.

"That's Jerry's one joke, Hunt," the chief ranger explained. "He works it off on everybody." He laid aside his stiff-brimmed hat, revealing a heavy shock of sandy hair with threads of gray at the temples.

"It isn't a joke," objected Straker. "Lots of people, especially women, aren't really interested; they just say yes to be agreeable when I point out that house that ain't there. No use showing them anything else, of course. If they don't see the house and admit it, then I know what else to point out. A woman who was up here in a party last week couldn't see it either, and said so. Husband was a newspaper man. Think she must have been French. There wasn't much to go on, except just the way she said things. Nearly wore my arm off after that pointing out things she was interested to see."

"Character guide, your little trick," said Rogers, grinning.

"I guess you'd call it that. The beauty of it is if they say they see the house, then that's all there is to it. I don't tell 'em it ain't there, and I just quit pointing out things."

"What we came up about, Jerry, is something else," Plummer said. "We can look at scenery some other time. Professor Rogers is inquiring into a matter with me. He's an old friend. The professor here of late has gained quite a reputation as an investigator into criminal matters—"

"Oh, a detective." Jerry Straker's eyes shifted quickly.

"Ordinarily it's just an avocation—when something interests me," Rogers said.

"I'd say from the results, Hunt, that it was more than that."

"What's on your mind, Floyd?" Straker interrupted bluntly.

"It's that mystery we've been trying to solve."

"Oh, you mean the fellow that the girl from Camp Curry found in Lost Valley—what there was left of him."

"Yes."

"What about it?"

"That's why we're here."

"Sit down. No use standing up." The fire lookout pointed to the chairs and sat down himself on the gray blanket of his cot. "What do I know about that?"

"Have you got a theory who the fellow might have been? One of the boys at the rangers' club last night was saying that you were wondering if he wasn't somebody you'd seen before."

"Well, now, I'll tell you, Floyd, about that. When I was at headquarters the other day I saw the stuff they found. You showed it to me yourself. It didn't mean anything then. But I got to thinking afterward when I got back up here that maybe I had seen the fellow. I hadn't made up my mind yet that it was worth speaking to you about. But I happened to mention what I was thinking to Bob Cole who was up yesterday—"

"It was Bob who was telling me."

"Oh—well, the fellow I have in mind came hiking up the mountain last fall. Early part of September."

"September?" Rogers interjected.

"Early part of September, as I was saying," Straker went on. "He was a fellow maybe thirty-five, or so. He didn't have much to say, and he was traveling a bit light. Left his pack down at the foot of the stairs, but it didn't look as though he carried much. He'd hiked up the old loggin' railroad. Only questions he asked was about the Tioga Road, and when would the pass be snowed in. When he left all he said was that he guessed he'd better go down to the Valley floor."

"Did he sign the register?"

"He wasn't going to, Floyd. But I told him he had to. I never looked to see what his name was, though. Always had a suspicion that he put down a fictitious name."

Straker got up from the cot and walked to the window ledge. He returned with the visitors' register and sat down again.

"September seventh it was, last year." He looked up at Rogers from the open book. "I can't read it. Take a look at it, Floyd." He passed the register to the chief ranger, who studied the signature.

"It could be Watkins, or Watson, or Wilkins. It begins with a 'W.' That's all you can be certain about. And the first name might be anything."

Rogers shook his head. "Doesn't check. The fellow I'm interested in is named Hugh Buckingham."

"Well, I thought at the time he didn't want me to know his right name. You get hunches." Jerry Straker's brows gathered in a frown. "Would an artist carry around his paint in a little flat box, something like a cigar box?" He looked at Rogers.

"Yes, why?"

"Well, among the things down at government center is a tube of some kind of paint, yellow ochre, I think. Must have belonged to the dead man. This fellow carried up a little box—flat like—" He measured with his large hands. "The reason I took it to be a painter's box was that a couple weeks before that there'd been a painter up here— at least, he said he was a painter. He had a little paint box like that. Sort of smeared up on the outside with paint. Said he was sketching."

"Would you recognize this Watson or Wilkins fellow from a photograph?" Rogers inquired suddenly. He reached into an inside pocket.

"I don't know if I would or wouldn't, Professor."

Rogers shuffled several unmounted photographs and gave two of them to Straker. The latter held them before his eyes. His lips thinned a little with concentration. Presently he handed one of the photographs back.

"I wouldn't recognize him in that picture. But this other one—I always look at a man's eyes. That's where he lives. A man's eyes is the man, I've always said. I don't forget eyes I've once had a good look at."

"You recognize him, then?" Rogers inquired.

"Yes, this is the fellow. I had quite a time getting a good look at his eyes, though. He just wouldn't give me a square look."

"What did he want to know about the Tioga Road and the pass?"

"Just what I told you a minute ago, Professor. Wanted to know what time of the year the pass would likely be closed by snow. And, I remember now, he wanted to know if he could hike up to the Tioga Road from the Valley floor in Yosemite without coming back up around this way. I told him there was a good trail and that there were camps still open at Merced Lake and Tuolumne Meadows where he could eat and sleep. But somehow I just thought he asked that last question just to be asking something."

"You think he wasn't really interested in the information?"

"No. He was just talking." Straker looked intently at Rogers. "Do you think you've got the dead man identified?"

"I wouldn't go that far." Rogers was momentarily silent. "It seems certain that the man I'm interested in is the man who was here at the lookout. But the date's wrong. There's not sufficient evidence down at government center to make it definite that the dead man and the fellow who was here at the fire lookout are the same person."

"How about the dentists? Don't they have a way of checking up, if you can find the right dentist?"

"Yes," said the chief ranger. "This fellow we found had had some dental work done. We're checking it down in the Bay area."

"Well, I'm sorry, Professor, that I can't help you out any more than I have," said Straker.

"On the contrary. You've been a real help, Mr. Straker."

"But you don't think this Watkins fellow and the dead man are the same, though."

"I don't say that. All that can be said now is that it's not conclusive. There's a strong presumption that the dead man is Buckingham; and there's no doubt that he was here on the date you say he was, and that he signed the register with a fictitious name."

"Well—" the chief ranger got up. "That's about the story, then, isn't it, Hunt?"

"I think so. Unless Mr. Straker can recall something else."

"I'm afraid I can't add anything. If I do happen to remember any more, I'll get in touch with you. Where will you be, Professor?"

"Floyd will know where I am. I'll probably be in the park for a while. I came up for a little rest and relaxation, as a matter of fact. Except that I did have this fellow Buckingham on my mind."

2

SUPERINTENDENT HAVERLY touched the switch of the inter-office communication system on his desk and spoke quietly, his head turned toward the black box. "Send Bruce Milbank in now," he said. Then he signed a letter he had just been reading and dropped it into the tray of outgoing mail. The door opened promptly and the trim, neatly uniformed figure of the assistant park naturalist entered.

"Come in, Bruce. Sit down."

The superintendent leaned back in his chair. The young man sat down and put his stiff-brimmed hat upon the broad desk top.

"You sent for me, sir?"

"Yes."

Superintendent Haverly was approaching middle age, but he possessed the vigor of a man much younger. His dark hair was tinged with gray, but his eyes were bright, his muscles hard. If need be he could take the trail in the high country and out-hike any of his rangers. Physical fitness was gospel with him. Personally he'd rather be out on the trail, but his years and experience required that he now spend most of his time at a desk.

There had been growing in him of late a feeling of dismay at the lazy habits of vacationers. They came in swarms, by the hundreds of thousands, each year to Yosemite. They drove about on the Valley floor, maybe fished a little, or rode bicycles; if they thought of it they visited the Museum; they danced, saw the free entertainment and the fire fall at night, probably wishing it were a night club instead, and then went home thinking they had seen the park. In truth they had spent their time in some seven square miles of wonderland, whereas there was more than a thousand square miles of high country, with even greater things to see and enjoy. There was rugged health to be earned by hard hiking on the mountain trails—

"You sent for me, sir?"

"Oh, yes. Excuse me, Bruce. My mind was wandering, I guess." The superintendent picked up a typewritten list from his blotter. "About the loop trail party Monday. The list is complete. Most of the members already have arrived, I think. One woman, though, a Miss Sherman, won't get here until Sunday night. You know what that means, of course—starting soft on a seventy-mile hike. I hope you won't be taping blistered heels all the way around."

Bruce Milbank grinned. "I hope not, sir."

"There's one other, I think, to speak about, a man named Turley. He's staying at the Ahwahnee." He consulted a memorandum. "No, I'm wrong about him. There was some uncertainty about his going, but it's definite now that he is."

Superintendent Haverly leaned across his desk and extended the list to the naturalist, who took it and glanced down the length of the page.

"Only thirteen?" He looked up at the superintendent.

"There was a cancellation—fortunately."

"Fortunately?"

"That's what I wanted to talk to you about."

"Yes, sir."

"Officially the number of hikers starting from Happy

Isles is thirteen. There's another one who will pick you up somewhere en route probably. You may not see him for a day or two. Or he may join you the first night at Merced Lake and go all the way around with you. He's already taken the trail. You won't have to watch out for him. He's an experienced hiker."

"Sounds a bit—unusual, sir."

"You were going to say mysterious, Bruce."

Milbank grinned slowly. Superintendent Haverly had a way of reading a man's mind, and the naturalist now admitted that he thought it was mysterious.

"Well, it is. Your unorthodox hiker, so to call him, is a fellow named Rogers—Huntoon Rogers. Professor of English in the University."

"I met him over at the rangers' club—with Mr. Plummer. He was talking with some of the boys. Does it—?"

"It all has to do with that fellow who was found in Lost Valley. Professor Rogers has come up to the park for a little vacation. He's an old friend of Plummer's. It's Plummer's idea that the professor might give us a hand, since we're not solving the mystery any too fast by ourselves. Professor Rogers has quite a reputation for such things."

"And this, of course, is all between ourselves? I mean about what the professor is up to?"

"Yes, naturally. When and if you run across him in the back country, he's just a lone hiker on his own. If he joins your party, make no objection. And, of course, keep everything to yourself. If he cares to do any explaining, that's his business. Understood?"

"Yes, sir." Milbank once more consulted the list. "I see Thomas Fulton's name here. Is he *the* Tommy Fulton?" Milbank's eyes sought his chief's face inquiringly.

"That's *the* Tommy Fulton. Surprised?"

"Yes, I am. But——he's past eighty, Mr. Haverly. Do you think a man that old can walk seventy miles and climb over Vogelsang Pass, and all that?"

"You'll be still more surprised, I think, Bruce. I had dinner with Mr. Fulton at the Ahwahnee last night. He's as enthusiastic as a boy of seventeen would be over this trip."

"But I thought he'd come to the hotel to retire and just read old books, and listen to his phonograph records. That's what he told me once. He had no future and, therefore, no further interest in what was ahead; he'd lived his life, and he'd come to the one spot he liked, just to live over the things that had gone before."

Superintendent Haverly laughed softly. "Yes, I know. He put it this way to me once: He had sat down at sunset to look back over the trail he had come. But he first spoke to me of this hiking trip several months ago. And he's been hardening himself with long walks and some hiking. He says he wants to see the High Sierras on foot before he dies. So, keep an eye out for the old fellow, Bruce. Use judgment. Don't pamper him, though, and hurt his feelings. Help him, of course, if he needs it. And if he shouldn't be able to make it, it will show up on him by the time you reach Tuolumne Meadows. He could come back by car from there on the Tioga Road."

"Yes, sir. I hope, though, for his sake that he makes it, and enjoys the hike."

There was a moment's silence which the subdued but steady roar of near-by Yosemite Falls filled in. The superintendent studied the young man's face. It was a lean face tanned by the sun; the chin was firm, the gray eyes clear and bright.

"Was there anything else, sir?"

"That's all, Bruce. Good luck. I hope nothing untoward happens."

"Yes, sir." The gray eyes searched the superintendent's face as if they would penetrate behind the remark to the reason for it. But instead of asking what was on the tip of his tongue to say, Bruce Milbank got to his feet, picked up his hat and turned toward the door. "Good-bye, sir."

"Good-bye, Bruce."

Superintendent Haverly sat relaxed in his chair for a moment, then leaned forward to touch the switch on his communication box.

"Has Plummer come in yet?" he asked. A voice answered in the negative. "As soon as he comes, ask him to come see me."

The superintendent sat back again. He wondered if he should have said quite as much as he did to Milbank— about any untoward happenings. The naturalist had got his thought, of course, but had not requested any explanation; in fact, he had ignored it altogether. He was glad it was Milbank who was in charge of the party. Milbank was an unusually reliable young man, and he always got on well with the hikers in the back country. If anything did happen he would know what to do.

But what could happen? That was it. That was what worried the superintendent. He felt a personal responsibility for every individual in Yosemite; he was a sort of super host to the hundreds of thousands who came every year to enjoy the park. Their welfare as well as their happiness was in his hands, although the vast majority came and went without realizing that he was there and what he was trying to do for them. He wanted more and more of these thousands to see the back country. The Valley floor, of course, was a never-ending source of enjoyment to all who came, but in the high country the trails, the many lakes, the timbered slopes, the solitude, the sunrises and sunsets which left one without words at such unimagined beauty was what he wanted the people to see. The weekly hiking parties was only a beginning; he hoped their numbers would grow; he schemed and planned so that more individuals and families and groups of boys and girls could be induced to shoulder a light pack and push out on their own—

"Mr. Plummer is coming in, sir," said the secretary's voice in the black box.

The door opened and the chief ranger entered.

"Come in, Floyd. Sit down."

"Sorry, I was delayed a little. I've just come from Happy Isles. Professor Rogers got off a few minutes ago."

"That's what I wanted to see you about."

"He said he'd like at least a day up around Lost Valley before the hiking party came along."

"What did Jerry Straker have of interest this morning?"

"Almost an identification. The fellow Rogers is looking for was at Trumbull Peak last year—September seventh. Fellow named Hugh Buckingham. Straker identified a photograph Rogers had. The register, though, was signed with a fictitious name."

"So there's a possibility, then, that the dead man's name was Hugh Buckingham?"

"Yes and no."

"How do you mean, Floyd?"

"Well, in the state the remains were in, about the only conclusive proof would be dental. But nothing has come in yet on that."

The superintendent leaned back in his chair, clasped his hands behind his head, and looked at the ceiling.

"In other words, Rogers is on the track of some fellow whose name is Hugh Buckingham, who was at Trumbull Peak September seventh; and last week we find the body of a man, dead many months, whose name might have been Buckingham, or again just plain Joe Doaks."

"Precisely."

"And will we ever know?"

"There you've got me." The chief ranger flung back in his chair. He ran his hand through his sandy hair and regarded the superintendent gravely.

"And how does this loop trail party of ours fit into the picture as Rogers sees it?"

"Well, Boss, I suspect you know more about that than I do. My ignorance is total. He did say this morning, as we were driving down from Trumbull Peak, that he believed he could smell a mystery before it happened."

"Humph! Odd, isn't it? All I know," said Superintendent Haverly, "is that I had a request from San Francisco to assist Professor Rogers in any way we could. Since he thinks he might like to join the hike, he can join it, of course. Now, that's between you and me, Floyd."

"Yes, sir. I gathered that he was doing something important—for the government. But whether it was Army or Navy, or F.B.I., he didn't say. Just between us, though—" Plummer drew close to the Superintendent, "it's got something to do with Japanese agents."

"If Professor Rogers could have taken us a little more into his confidence, we would have been spared conjectures at what to expect." The superintendent was not so much critical as curious as to what might be going on. He reflected upon the information the chief ranger had imparted.

"Hunt is a bit of an odd sort, Boss," Plummer said, as if his friend required an explanation. "He doesn't talk much about his hobby. It is a hobby, definitely. Teaching is really his profession.

"But he's done some brilliant work in criminology. I couldn't name off hand all the cases he's solved in the past seven or eight years. But I know he's had a lot of them here on the West Coast, and down into Mexico even—and as far out as Hawaii.

"I don't think he ever took any pay for anything he did, either. He's not even interested in the credit for what he does. He'd just as soon let some sleuth in the police department take the bow when it's all over."

"He is an odd sort, isn't he?"

"You told Milbank about Rogers?"

"All I knew to tell him. I couldn't warn him, if he should have been warned, because what is there to warn him against? Bruce is a steady man. I'm thankful that it's he who is taking the party around the loop."

"Bruce is equal to any emergency."

"That's what I tell myself."

"Look here, Boss. This thing isn't getting on your nerves, I hope. If you'll permit me to remind you—as I've done before—you're too conscientious. No human being can foresee the manner and the moment when some one of the thousands who come to this park will get himself clawed by a bear, or fall two or three thousand feet down onto the

Valley floor, or lay himself open to some other such trouble
—and I don't think it's wise to try."

"I know. Thanks for reminding me, Floyd. I'll try to
forget it as much as I can. I'm due for the weekend down
in San Francisco." He looked at his wristwatch. "I've still
got an hour or so before I start. Nothing can happen before
I get back Monday evening. If you need to get in touch
with me, you know where to call."

"But try to forget it, Boss. I'll do my best to keep things
on an even keel until you get back. Oh, I've got one of the
girls over at the park company headquarters looking back
through the files of last September to see if she can find a
registration card for this man Buckingham. Jerry said
that when the fellow left Trumbull Peak he volunteered
that he was hiking down to the Valley floor."

"But if he signed with a fictitious name——"

"That's what makes it a tough job. The name on Jerry's
register might be Wilson or Watson or Wilkins. The 'W'
is about the only thing sure in the signature. But down
here, of course, he might have signed a name beginning
with 'J' or 'S.' "

"Sort of hopeless, isn't it?"

"Maybe."

"Did I tell you that old Tommy Fulton is going on the
hike?"

"That old man!"

"Yes, that old man. Past eighty."

"Is it safe to let him start?"

"I think so. He could go all the way around just on his
enthusiasm, but there's more to him than that, despite
his years."

"Interesting old chap. Had a stormy career—domestically, I understand. I don't know how true it is, but the new manager up at the hotel was telling me that there was more or less uproar with first one and then another of his wives. Kids were wild and expensive too. It went on for years. I can understand why the man might want to spend the few years left to him amid the peace and quiet of Yosemite. I'd like to do the same thing when I get that far along on the road, although my own domestic life has been as smooth as the surface of Mirror Lake; I'd like to spend it right here in a little cabin among the big trees at the edge of the meadow where the deer come to feed."

"The park sort of gets hold of you, doesn't it?" The superintendent smiled at his chief ranger.

"It does. That's why I've always contended that primitive man has had the best of us civilized moderns. Here we can see it; down in San Francisco, say, you only realize that something's wrong with life, and you don't know what it is."

"Well—" Superintendent Haverly glanced at his watch once more and sat forward in his chair. "I wish, Floyd, we could sit around the rest of the afternoon and talk, but I'm afraid I'll have to do a little more work before I go."

The chief ranger got up, put on his hat, and reached for the doorknob. "Well, a pleasant trip, Boss. And don't worry about Yosemite while you're gone. It'll still be here when you get back. It will be here a hundred thousand years from now. That's what I tell myself when I get to stewing about things."

3

CLAUDIA BENSON paid her check at the cafeteria and went outside into the fresh cool air. The breakfast queue of hungry vacationers, waiting their turn to eat, still extended along the sidewalk, a mixture of humanity attired in slacks and jeans, sports shirts, and gay sweaters, with scarcely a skirt or a well-pressed suit of clothes to be seen. She was reminded of a quotation which she thought was from an old hymn; it was something about where every prospect pleases and only man is vile. She glanced up at the gray towering mass of Half Dome which soared more than four thousand feet almost straight up from the narrow Valley floor. She was going to get away from humanity, humanity in the mass, for a whole week. She was going to hike and climb, and breathe high mountain air and forget San Francisco, and the office, clanging street cars, crowded elevators and jammed lunch counters.

She looked at her wristwatch as she hurried along the walk to her tent among the trees. Here she was pushing again, hurrying, just as she did in town, all keyed up and tense. With a deliberate effort she changed to an easier, longer stride, and breathed deeply of the pine-scented air. It was almost an hour before she was due at Happy Isles, and it was only a mile. But she'd get her pack from her tent and be on her way. She had put her suitcase in her car and locked it before breakfast, and the car would stay in the parking lot until she got back.

Some children were playing about in the heavy carpet

of pine needles as Claudia left the sidewalk and turned down the row of tents to where her own was pitched. A few disheveled late risers were on their way to the washrooms when she stopped before her tent. A Steller Jay, his crest erect, hopped stiff-legged away from the raised step with something he had found to eat, soared with a flash of blue into a tree, and continued madly leaping upward from branch to branch around the tree trunk until he disappeared from view.

Claudia went inside the tent. Her pack was lying on the bed as she had left it. Nothing had been molested in her absence. She retouched her lips before the mirror, and put her compact in a pocket of her gray whipcord breeches. She patted the pocket where she carried her money. For safety a handkerchief was stuffed in on top. Before the mirror she gave a more rakish twist to the soft light brown felt hat, pushed a curl into place and was ready.

She picked up her pack from the bed, and then put it down. She wondered what was wrong with it, for it was strapped together just as she had left it. Or was it? With a feeling of vague apprehension she undid the straps, and unrolled it. Hastily turning through it, though, she found everything as it should be—an extra beige sweater, an extra pair of wool socks, an extra lumberjack shirt, her first aid kit, underwear, and toilet articles.

Funny, she thought, as she rolled the pack together again and buckled the straps; she'd had the oddest little feeling of a sudden that something was wrong, but it wasn't. City nerves, she guessed as she pushed the tent flap aside, stepped down from the wooden tent floor to the step, and then off into the pine needles and turned in the direction of Happy Isles, where the hiking party was to rendezvous.

As she swung leisurely along the hard path she heard footsteps behind her, hurrying footsteps as if someone was bent on overtaking her.

"Oh, I say! Young lady!"

Claudia stopped and looked back. A matronly figure in faded jeans and brown cardigan, with her head tied up in a red and yellow scarf, was approaching.

"You look like one of the hikers." A beaming smile spread over the broad plain face.

"Yes?"

"So am I. Are you going on the seven-day hike?"

"Yes." A sinking feeling assailed Claudia's stomach.

"I'm Beryl Lindsay. Isn't it nice to run into you like this? I don't know a soul who's going. What did you say your name is?"

"Claudia Benson."

"I'm from Oklahoma. I teach a school in Bushyhead. I got in just yesterday afternoon by bus. Isn't it wonderful! It's my first visit to Yosemite. There was the cutest little deer, a fawn and its mother, right in front of my tent when I came away just now. And is that—" she twisted her head to the right and stared up through the trees. "Why, it's almost unbelievable—that rock wall there. You can hardly see the top of it."

"You're looking up at Glacier Point, three thousand feet above Camp Curry," said Claudia, feeling like the conductor of a rubberneck excursion.

"Oh, look! That robin! Or is it a robin?"

"Yes, that's a robin."

"But he looks sort of rusty and faded."

"That's the western robin. He's a mountain dweller.

You don't often see him at low levels."

They walked on together. For a few moments neither spoke. Claudia was a trifle depressed. She wondered if the party would be made up of school teachers. She wondered if everybody would start off hating each other. It was a strain to have to live a week with complete strangers. She recalled, though, what a ranger had told her the year before when he urged her to take the hike.

"Why, the last night or two, nobody wants to go to bed. They hate to break up; they sit around and talk and sing songs. They don't want the trip to come to an end."

She had her fingers crossed. Then she caught herself up sharply. Why should she nurse an attitude like that on a hiking trip? You got to disliking people down in the city; you became critical of everybody. There wasn't any give and take down there; you harbored grudges and resented slights and elbowed people in crowds. That's what she had wanted to get away from. That was why she was in Yo-semite.

"I'm a secretary in San Francisco," she confided in a burst of synthetic fellow feeling to Miss Lindsay. "I work in a law office."

"How interesting!"

"I'm hoping there will be an agreeable crowd. You really never know on a hike like this, though."

"I get along with people beautifully. People are my hobby. I like them. I make a study of them."

Claudia did her best to be agreeable. She answered many questions about the trees and the birds as they walked along, for Beryl Lindsay seemed to possess one of those sponge-like minds that sopped up information like water, and Claudia, who had long been familiar with Yosemite, could answer most of her questions.

The sound of rushing water as it poured over countless stones in the rocky river bed became ever louder as they approached the rendezvous. The sidewalk and the parallel road came to an end in a grove of trees. Several cars were parked, and people were standing or idling about. Some obviously were not hikers. Claudia made out a small group clustered about a ranger near a rustic bridge, and they went over to it.

"I'm Bruce Milbank," said the neatly uniformed young man, lifting his hat to Claudia and Miss Lindsay. "You're going on the seven-day hike?"

"Yes," answered Claudia. She introduced her companion and gave him her own name, and Milbank checked them on his list.

"Only two or three more to come," he said, smiling. "Some of the party already have started on the trail. There's still ten minutes before we're scheduled to leave. Of course, now, time—" he lifted his voice so that all might hear—"time isn't everything on this hike, ladies and gentlemen. The point is nothing has to be done exactly on the dot. We're due at various camps for the night. We're due back on the Valley floor in seven days. So you can forget your watches. We don't have to catch any trains or busses. And, since most of us are here now, I might as well say that I'm not delivering any set lectures about the wonders of Yosemite. I'm not a school master, nor a chaperon, except in a very general sense. But I am here with you on this trip to see that you enjoy yourselves. I'll try to answer any and all questions you may ask. I expect to point out many things of interest as we go along—and," Bruce Milbank winced inwardly, "if any of you get any blisters,

better tell me about it and I'll help fix you up. I hope you all
have comfortable shoes, because it's your feet, not mine,
that will suffer. And please—" he smiled deprecatingly,
and looked at Claudia, "this is personal—I'm not a forest
ranger. I'm an assistant park naturalist—"

"But—"

"Yes, Miss Lindsay?"

"I thought you were all forest rangers."

Bruce Milbank shook his head. He smiled. "The point
really isn't important. We have park naturalists, park
rangers, park foresters. There's a park photographer. We
all dress alike. Some of the boys are sensitive. I merely
mentioned it for the sake of accuracy. But call me anything
you like—just so it's pleasant."

Claudia Benson liked this tall, friendly young man in
his neat gray-green uniform and stiff-brimmed hat with
its leather hatband. His eyes were gray; she liked his ready,
friendly smile. Best of all she liked the sense of relaxation
which he seemed to project against the background of the
noisy stream. Milbank was in no hurry to start. It was
near the scheduled time, but he wasn't fretting because
several of the party hadn't arrived yet.

"If any of you want to start on ahead, we'll catch up
with you," he added. "Don't push, though; remember it's
twelve miles and a little over to tonight's camp."

Several of the party began to move off along the trail.
A thin, spare figure leaning against a tree trunk stood up
straight and swung a pack upon his shoulders. A black felt
hat was pulled down upon his forehead. He came toward
Claudia and Miss Lindsay.

"My name's Fulton," he said. "Either of you girls want
to start on ahead with me? Or both of you?" He smiled,

showing yellowing crooked teeth.

Beryl Lindsay accepted with alacrity. Claudia felt relieved at this separation from her newly acquired companion. Mr. Fulton looked like a nice old man. But he seemed awfully old for the trip.

"I'll catch up with you," Claudia said as they started off.

A few yards away a man sat on the ground with his back against the trunk of a small tree, his pack on the ground beside him. He was smoking a cigarette and apparently looking at something far away among the trees. A strange feeling coursed through Claudia. She couldn't see the man's face, but something about the crisp brown hair, the curve of his cheek was familiar. She had a sinking feeling in the pit of her stomach, and she remembered Yosemite when everything was covered with snow and skis were flashing on the slopes at Badger Pass.

"Are you all right, Miss Benson?" Bruce Milbank asked of a sudden.

"Yes—of course. Yes, I'm all right. Why?"

"Sorry. For a moment I thought you looked as though you didn't feel well."

"I'm quite all right," said Claudia. She didn't mean to make her tone so sharp. She turned about and faced the naturalist.

"I'm sorry—"

"Is Douglas Kramer a member of this hiking party?"

"Yes." Milbank fluttered the list in his hand. "His name's here."

Claudia started away from the group toward the sidewalk to Camp Curry, swinging her pack by a strap. She kicked viciously at a small stone in her path. There was a roaring in her ears that was not of the rushing stream pouring over the rocks at Happy Isles.

"Miss Benson!" Milbank's voice was raised a trifle. "Miss Benson, where are you going?"

She didn't answer, but continued stubbornly onward. She had turned her back on the whole thing. If Doug Kramer was going—

She heard a scuffling of determined footsteps near her, and a khaki-clad pair of legs crossed her path. She looked up to see Douglas Kramer blocking her way.

"Now, see here, Claudia," he said firmly.

"Get out of my way, please," she said.

Kramer seized her by the arm. It was useless to struggle in his grip.

"Now, listen here," he said bluntly. "Don't be a little fool. Until you showed up here five minutes ago, I didn't know you were in Yosemite."

"I'm not interested in what you know or don't know."

"Until five minutes ago I thought you were still down in San Francisco slaving at that job. I swear that when I made my reservation for this trip I hadn't the slightest notion that you were planning to go too. I certainly wouldn't have come here, if I had known it."

"I'm still not interested in what you're saying."

"What are you going to do?"

"I'm not going on this hike. I'm getting out of the park as fast as I can go."

"You're not doing anything of the kind. If anybody kicks out of the party, I'll kick out."

He still held a firm grip on her arm. She tried suddenly to jerk free, but his strength was too great. She had never hated anybody so much in all her life as she hated Douglas Kramer now. He had followed her up here. She didn't believe a word he said. As they stood tensely together, Milbank strolled over to them.

"I say," he began, "is this a private fight, or can I have a pair of gloves and get in too?"

Something happened inside of Claudia. It was as though cold water had been thrown over her; her eyes cleared and things were not so blurred with anger as they had been.

"Careful, Ranger," said Kramer slowly. "This is strictly a private argument."

Still Milbank didn't go; he stood smiling at both of them. Claudia suddenly spoke up.

"He says he'll leave the party if I go along."

"Pardon me, Ranger, but the young lady is wrong. I didn't say I'd leave the party if she went along. I told her that if either of us were to withdraw, it would be I."

"Miss Benson, shouldn't you think it over?" suggested Milbank.

Claudia had suddenly made up her mind. She was being a bit of a fool. That was the last thing in the world she intended to be in the eyes of Douglas Kramer; she wouldn't give him the satisfaction of knowing that she had been foolish enough to withdraw from the party, or to force him to do so. The back country was big enough for both of them; she didn't have to talk to him. She'd ignore him.

"I've changed my mind, Mr. Milbank," she said quite calmly.

"And you're going?"

"Yes."

"How about you, Mr. Kramer?"

"I've been counting on this trip for a long time."

"That's fine."

A man and a woman dressed in hiking clothes, each carrying a sizable pack, crowded into the small group.

"Are you the guide for the hiking party?" asked the man.

"Yes, sir."

"My name's Al DeWitt. This is Mrs. DeWitt. We were afraid we wouldn't get here in time."

Milbank shook hands with them and introduced them to Claudia and Kramer.

"We're ready to start, as soon as one more man shows up. A Mr. William Turley," he said.

A quiet-spoken, dark-complexioned man near the naturalist's elbow opened his lips.

"My name's Turley."

"Then you're here too! I didn't see you come."

"I drove up a few minutes ago. My car's over there." He pointed to the cars parked in the grove of trees.

"All right, folks." Milbank turned and called to the remaining members of the party. "Everybody's here. Let's hit the trail."

4

THIS was the second season for Bruce Milbank as guide for the hiking parties on the loop trail trip, and this was the second trip this year. He wondered a bit at what lay ahead; for somehow this trip was starting out differently from all the others. What looked like a lovers' quarrel had occurred at Happy Isles. There was one less hiker in the party, and somewhere ahead was a man who might or might not join the party, and he in some vague mysterious way was connected with the finding of a dead man.

The superintendent's attitude had puzzled him. Perhaps he should have asked for more details when he got his final instructions, but he had thought it best not to. If there was anything of which he should have been informed he would have been told—that is, if Mr. Haverly knew. That was the point; the superintendent seemed in the dark himself. Being of a practical nature, however, Bruce Milbank dismissed the matter from his mind. There were more immediate things to be concerned with. Blisters would develop, as well as amateur ornithologists, botanists, and geologists. He'd have to get them all together at some time, probably at lunch, and tell them how Yosemite Valley was formed. That was a fundamental.

Milbank moved ahead along the trail, passing several pairs in the party. He overtook a woman who had interested him earlier. She had been among the first at the rendezvous. She now swung along with an easy stride, using a stick she had found for a cane. Her gray tweed skirt was expensive, as was the light green sweater. It was difficult to guess her age, and he didn't try.

"You look as if you had done this sort of thing before, Miss Forbes," he said.

"Yes. Where haven't I walked on this earth?" she countered.

"Really?"

"I cut my teeth on English walking tours when I was just a kid. And I've hiked somewhere else almost every year since. And I'm no spring chicken, either." She smiled a curiously twisted little smile when she said it. Her lips were unusually mobile and expressive.

"Then I don't need worry about you."

"Not at all, Mr. Milbank. Tell me, though—there's a man up ahead, a big fellow wearing a gray sweat shirt and a sort of an Alpine hat. He has a very toothy smile—"

"Harry Hodges?"

"Oh. Could I be mistaken in the name?"

It was spoken as if she were talking to herself. Milbank looked at her oddly, and Miss Forbes' brown eyes seemed to twinkle.

"I'll tell you the story some time. It's too long now. But confirm something for me—a bit of weather lore, I guess you'd call it. Maybe it's just ranger lore."

"Yes?"

"Somebody was saying that when the snow all disappears from Half Dome it's a sign that all the trails are open in the high country. Is that true?"

"That's a rule of thumb we go by, yes."

"Isn't that interesting!"

They walked on together. The sound of rushing water was ever present, while in the background was the growing roar of the falls that lay ahead of them. The trail grew steeper. Milbank was silent, wondering what other mystery figure he had on this party; he wished he might probe behind Miss Forbes' remark about Hodges, but he didn't feel that he should do so at the moment. She might just as well have said: "Why is that fellow traveling under another name?" It was implicit in her manner although her words didn't convey as much.

"You know," he said to Miss Forbes, "no two hiking parties are ever the same. You might think that some fourteen or fifteen people getting together for a whole week with the common urge to hike in the high country might run to type—"

"And they don't?"

"The only thing they seem to have in common is the urge. They may be as wide as the poles apart in everything else."

"I should think that would make it very interesting for you."

"It does."

"There's another man up front somewhere," said Miss Forbes experimentally.

"Yes?"

"His name is Leon Mullins."

"I have him listed under that name."

Miss Forbes ignored the subtlety Milbank put into the statement.

"He's a cowboy, or was for the greater part of his early life. Then he got fancy and began to play the dude ranch circuit, if you get what I mean. And he always saved his money."

"You'd think he'd go in for the saddle trip. They say a

cowboy never walks if he can ride a horse."

"That's something else that's funny too," said Miss Forbes. "You know, I've been around quite a lot. I've visited at one time or another practically every country worth seeing. You can't help running into somebody you've met before, if you travel much. Mr. Mullins is trying to puzzle me out—who I am and where he's seen me before. I'm not saying anything yet."

Milbank would have liked to continue this conversation, but waiting on the trail was a young woman with a flower for him to identify. Miss Forbes walked on.

"Indian paint brush. Interested in botany, Miss Sherman?"

"Not exactly. But it's so lovely and delicate. I sing."

"Oh."

"On the radio. I used to dub voices in Hollywood, though."

"That's interesting."

"But I didn't like it. I was always somebody else's voice, you know. The audience heard me but never saw me, and some so-called singing star would get credit for what I did. I couldn't see it. I'm ambitious to go places. Is that the roar of the falls we hear now?"

"Yes. It's not far. Trail steep for you?"

"No, I like to climb."

Milbank looked at her shoes dubiously but said nothing. He'd asked her before they started from Happy Isles if they were comfortable. He hadn't seen anything more of either of the two young people who had quarreled at the start until he came up to Kramer sitting beside the trail. Kramer looked at Miss Sherman.

"Hello," he said.

"Hello."

Milbank went on, leaving the two together. Hiking parties had a way of starting out sort of hit or miss. They didn't really shake down until after they got by both the Vernal and the Nevada falls. As a rule the members were curious about each other and devised various stratagems, all of which Milbank was familiar with, to find out who their fellow hikers were. There was the direct approach, such as Douglas Kramer was using with Miss Sherman. There was the method of Miss Forbes. Only in her case, she already knew more about the two men she had mentioned than she was willing to admit.

The hikers climbed steadily onward between the steep walls of Merced Canyon, paused in turn at each of the roaring cascades of water thundering down upon the rocks below, and entered Little Yosemite Valley with its heavy growth of cedar and fir, its meadows now filled with wildflowers. Milbank had got the hikers together now, strung out on the trail behind him. Without his having to remind them, they had become conscious of the fact that this day's hike was one of spectacular interest. They were forgetting themselves in the midst of an abundant nature; the mountain air, the vigorous exercise, the new world of interest for roving eyes always did something to people. It was working on this party as it had upon others that he had guided along the high trails.

Immediately behind him now walked Thomas Fulton. The elderly man had taken the position as though it were his by right, as though he wanted all to see that he was walking strongly, that his legs were as good or better than the rest even though they had carried him about the earth for upward of eighty years.

Conversation dwindled. It was steady hiking now and still a long way to camp. Unused muscles were being called upon, reserves of strength were being tapped for the first time in months, years probably for some of the party. They passed out of the Little Yosemite Valley into Lost Valley. At last Milbank called a halt for a brief rest, and the hikers dropped to the ground, some with arms and legs outflung, others propped against rocks or tree trunks.

"Do you know why I came on this trip?" said Al DeWitt from his position against a tree, addressing no one in particular. He was a large reddish person, with soft muscles and a voice unusually high pitched.

"No," said Miss Lindsay. "Why?"

"To prove to my wife that I haven't forgotten how to walk. I was born in an automobile. Actually. On the way to the hospital in an ambulance. And May holds it against me. She says it's colored my whole life." He looked at his wife. "Ain't it so, honey?"

"We haven't finished the hike yet. We've just begun."

Milbank noted the hunched figure of a hiker on the ground somewhat apart from the others. He had the rugged features and strong spare build of a man who had lived out of doors all his life. He showed no signs of weariness as did the others. He wore a wide-brimmed, fawn-colored hat and square-toed, high-heel boots. The name Mullins popped into his mind. It was Leon Mullins who Miss Forbes had told him had been a cowboy in his early life. He remembered the name now.

Mullins had taken a seat on the ground from which he could see Miss Forbes' face. He stared at her from time to time. At the least sign Miss Forbes made of looking in his direction, his small blue eyes shifted instantly. Evidently Mullins still was striving to puzzle out who she was and where he had seen her before.

Harry Hodges, the second of the two men Miss Forbes had mentioned, lay on his back with arms and legs extended as if exhausted, his oddly shaped felt hat covering his face. He had been showing signs of fatigue. Hodges and Miss Sherman were the only two who seemed to be having difficulty. Claudia Benson and her school-teacher companion, Beryl Lindsay, were sitting together, the former plainly ignoring the existence of Douglas Kramer. They were tired but a long way from exhaustion.

So far so good, thought Milbank. The hikers were shaking down into a normal party after all. He wondered now at the concern he had felt at the outset, and why the superintendent's manner on the Saturday before had been so disturbing. He'd had some conversation with every member of the party by this time. There were three or four among the men who were still deep in their shells. Ralph Stoner was one; he was absorbed in fishing. He had carried his rod and tackle a great part of the way ready to try any likely pool he encountered. Hammond and Turley and Dudley—he referred to his list to make sure of the names—probably would shake down a little later. Wait until after dinner at Merced Lake, or possibly tomorrow's breakfast.

"Any blisters, Miss Sherman?" he addressed the radio singer.

She shook her head. "I don't think so."

"You were limping. Better take a look."

Beryl Lindsay near by rolled over on her side and elbow and gave a pull to the stout boot which Ruth Sherman unlaced. The sock came off, and the teacher seized a pink foot.

"She's got one on her heel, Mr. Milbank."

"Got any bandaids, Miss Sherman?" the naturalist inquired. He tried to be cheerfully casual as he reached for his first aid kit.

"I didn't think I'd need any. I never blister."

Milbank went across the open space to where she sat, squatted down and deftly taped the blister.

"Anybody else?" he inquired.

No one else required attention, and Milbank put away his kit. He had made no inquiries of old Mr. Fulton, for he didn't seem any more used up than the younger members of the party. He recalled the superintendent's warning, and so made no overtures that the old man might resent.

"I say, Bruce," the old man suddenly spoke up.

"Yes, Mr. Fulton?"

"Wasn't it here in Lost Valley somewhere that they found that dead man a couple of weeks ago?"

A silence broken only by the cry of a woodpecker ensued. A queer, bizarre note seemed to have been struck.

"A dead man?" echoed Miss Forbes.

Nobody ventured anything in response. Probably old Mr. Fulton was the only member of the party beside himself, thought Milbank, who had known about it. Why couldn't he have kept still?

"Here in this spot, you mean?" asked Beryl Lindsay.

"Farther back," Milbank answered. "We've already passed the place."

Al DeWitt sat up with interest. "Who was he? First I'd heard about it."

"Nobody seems to know," Fulton answered. "Superintendent Haverly told me Friday, when we had dinner together, that they didn't know who he was. Probably some lost hiker."

"How did he die?" Miss Forbes' interest mounted. "Was he murdered?"

Bruce Milbank, now that the subject had come out in the open, decided to tell what was known. "Who the man was and how he died haven't been discovered yet," he said. "Probably, as Mr. Fulton suggests, he was some hiker who died from accidental injuries, or from natural causes. He had been dead all winter." There was really very little to tell, for that was all he knew himself.

Douglas Kramer spoke when Milbank had finished. He undid his pack and took a dull, stained object from it. He tossed it on the ground at Milbank's feet.

"Here's something I found back there." He motioned with his head, indicating the trail they had traveled. "Off the trail a little bit—ten yards, maybe. Happened to kick it out of the pine needles."

"It's a knife!" said Claudia Benson.

Milbank picked it up and held it so that all might see. He turned it about. It was a hunting knife of a type any hiker might carry into the back country, and lose if he was careless. The heavy blade was stained with rust. In the horn handle two initials were scratched. He puzzled them out. One looked like an 'H,' the other like a 'B.' They meant nothing to him, however. He offered the knife to others who were interested. Several of the men looked at it. Miss Forbes was the only one among the women who would touch it. It came back to Milbank, who undid his pack and stowed it away.

"Well," he said, "we've got several miles to go. How about it, folks?"

5

LONG before they reached camp, Claudia Benson wished heartily that she had not started on the hike. Twelve miles—or was it fourteen?—was too much, even without a pack. Her pack got heavier and heavier, like her legs, over which she seemed to have no command; the latter seemed to move on their own without her willing it. The tireless swing of the legs clad in jeans ahead of her was hypnotic; she wondered how Beryl Lindsay could do it. They carried nearly twice as much weight as her own.

Somebody was always pointing out natural wonders— trees or rocks or birds. She wasn't interested. For a time the party moved like midget insects along the base of a huge glacier-scoured expanse of granite. And somebody had to point out that it was the largest area of its kind in North America. But Claudia didn't thrill to the fact as Miss Lindsay did.

At last they entered a grove of aspen, quiet and cool. Beyond it glistened the blue surface of a lake. Camp was not far away. The prospect did much to ease the irritation Claudia felt at Douglas Kramer's actions. Ever since the party had halted in Lost Valley he had been flirting with Ruth Sherman. The last two miles he carried her pack in addition to his own, helped her around and over obstacles which she was capable of surmounting unaided. Doug was doing it to annoy her. She was certain of it. Perhaps the irritation stimulated her to cover that last half mile. She arrived at the camp among the first, on the heels of Mr.

Fulton, who walked so fast at the finish that she could hardly keep up with him.

Claudia flung herself on the camp bed and lay like a fallen log. She didn't want to move for a week, maybe never again. She didn't know it was possible to be so tired, to have so many aching bones, to have her heart pound so steadily and so profoundly. That's all she was, a beating heart and an aching body, and a mind too weary to rest. She guessed she was softer than she had dreamed she could be. She wondered if maybe she'd better not go on. There were saddle horses in Yosemite, and they could send one up for her. She'd ride back to the Valley floor, that's what she would do. She couldn't walk any more. If she went on with the party there were still sixty miles to go. The mere thought was appalling.

Presently she realized that she wasn't the only one who suffered. She heard Mr. DeWitt groaning somewhere near by, and his wife alternately sympathizing and chiding. Except for the voices of the DeWitts there was a strange silence over the whole camp; bird cries seemed to sound in an otherwise empty world. Then outside Bruce Milbank began talking to a camp employee about bears. Another voice, which Claudia later learned belonged to the man who ran the camp, joined in. The bear that had been so troublesome about camp the year before hadn't come back. He'd been live-trapped and taken to a remote area of the park and released.

"You've only got thirteen in your party this time, Mr. Milbank. How come?" a voice said.

"There was a cancellation at the last minute."

"There's a fellow staying here at the camp last day or so. Was asking about when you'd get in. Kind of thought he figured on joining you—"

"That so?"

"Fellow named Rogers. Told him he didn't have a chance."

"Did he say he wanted to join us?"

"Didn't say so right out, but it's on his mind."

"Where is he?"

"He went off for a hike early in the afternoon."

The voices drifted away as Claudia dozed. When she wakened she felt completely empty inside; if it was hunger it was the sharpest hunger she'd ever felt. Every cell in her body seemed to crave food. She stretched tired muscles; they were stiff. She wondered when dinner would be served. She'd have to freshen up and put on makeup to repair the ravages of the hike. She feared that she would look twenty years older when she dared face a mirror.

She lay quietly for a long time. She thought of Harry Hodges, one of the hikers. He had walked with her for several miles, and had offered to carry her pack, but she hadn't let him. He was twice her age, but he had been a very pleasant companion, and thoughtful of the others. Once he had offered to carry old Mr. Fulton's pack, and had been curtly rebuffed. The old man must be quite sensitive. But the thing she remembered particularly was that Mr. Hodges hadn't resented it, but instead had been only amused. Claudia meant to talk more with the man, because he seemed quite interesting.

She rolled over. Knifelike stabs of pain struck the muscles of her legs and back. She got to her feet to see if she could stand, then sat down again and slowly massaged her stiffened muscles. Her pack lay on the floor where she had dropped it when she staggered to the bed. Finally she summoned courage enough to retrieve it and sat back on the edge of the bed with the pack beside her. She felt the awakening of confidence. She was going to be able to walk again!

The pack came open beside her as she undid the straps, and she unrolled it looking for her cold cream. Her face felt as if it had been burned black by the sun. An odd little piece of jade lay among her own things. It wasn't hers. She'd never seen it before and she couldn't imagine how it had got into her pack.

Claudia sat on the bed staring at the tent wall, trying to think. Somebody must have slipped it into her pack. She thought back over the long weary miles of the hike. None of the men had carried it, although the queer-looking Mr. Hammond had offered to do so. On the rest stops she had used it for a pillow. It seemed impossible for anyone to have slipped the piece of jade into her pack without her knowledge.

A little shiver went up Claudia's back when she recalled that that morning before she left Camp Curry she had thought for a moment that the pack had been disturbed while she was absent at breakfast. Was it possible that somebody had been in her tent while she was away and put the thing in her pack then? But, no, she'd unrolled her pack then and there was nothing unusual about it.

She stared at the piece of jade. It was not large. She could conceal it in her closed hand. The carving was delicately done. Some genius must have created it. The oddest little monkey face stared up into her own. It almost seemed as if it could speak. The monkey's figure was exquisitely proportioned. It sat arms relaxed, shoulders drooping, a weary and lonely little figure. But there was nothing to identify it. She couldn't explain it, and so she slipped the jade monkey into the pocket of her breeches and dismissed it from her mind.

The camp was stirring into life now; exhausted hikers had revived and were hungrily awaiting the dinner hour. Claudia went outside. The sun was down behind the peaks; rose tints already were creeping into the white granite masses that rimmed the wooded valley. The noisy nutcrackers down by the lake were drowning out all other bird sounds.

Miss Forbes sat smoking a cigarette, staring idly into space. When she discovered Claudia, she moved over and patted the bench beside her.

"Sit down." Her voice was warm and friendly. "How did you stand the hike?"

Claudia eased herself down upon the bench. "I'm just one colossal ache."

"You'll get over it."

"I hope so. Aren't you all tired out?"

"I keep in pretty good condition. At all times. I'm a little tired, naturally. Anybody would be after a hike like that. You see, we climbed nearly three thousand feet in addition to walking the twelve or thirteen miles from Happy Isles."

Maribel Forbes was a different type from Beryl Lindsay. The fact was even more evident to Claudia now. Miss Forbes didn't wear her humanity all on the outside; she hadn't barged up as though she had found a long-lost cousin, but instead sat back quietly and observed and appraised. Miss Forbes probably wrote or painted, or perhaps lectured. She might be a college dean. Her manner was distinguished; her features were strong and regular, and the gray in her hair was most becoming. She wasn't the type that would start out to walk seventy miles on mountain trails, and yet on second thought she was the very person to do that.

"When do we eat?" said Claudia.

"Six. It's about ten minutes yet. I came around here to get away from the odors of the kitchen. They only aggravate my hunger. Who is that man?"

A tall, broad-shouldered man came around the corner of the dining tent. He wore a leather jacket, and old khaki trousers tucked into the top of high laced boots. A battered felt hat was pulled down upon his forehead.

"I don't know," said Claudia.

"He showed up about half an hour ago. I didn't see him in our party today. Did you?"

"Oh! Why, I do know him too!"

"Who is he?"

Claudia got up from the bench, her face suddenly screwed up with the twinges of painful muscles.

"Professor Rogers!" she called.

Huntoon Rogers stopped, lifted his hat, then moved a few steps toward the bench. He held out his hand to Claudia.

"Now, wait a minute," he said, a smile lighting up his mild blue eyes. "I know you." He hesitated, searching Claudia's face. "You were in English 33b about three years ago. Miss—Miss—I've got it. You're Miss Benson. Claudia Benson."

"That's right."

They shook hands warmly.

"How do you remember us all? There are so many of us."

"I remember how well you played the part of Ophelia at the Campus Little Theatre."

"That was my last theatrical."

"I'm sorry. You'd have done well to go on."

"Oh, no. Not ever, Professor. Won't you come over and meet Miss Forbes?"

There was a rush, almost a scramble for the table when dinner was announced. Claudia found herself separated from Professor Rogers, who was at the end of the table with Miss Forbes. But there wasn't to be anything that could be called conversation; everybody was too hungry to talk.

"You knew that we stay over here at Merced Lake all day tomorrow, didn't you? To rest up." Mr. Hammond spoke to her as the dessert was being put on and the coffee cups re-filled. He had told her that afternoon that his name was Jack Hammond. Claudia had not been impressed with him; he ran to the gorilla type, for he was dark and hairy with long arms. His voice sounded as though it had been roughened with a file.

"I knew that, yes. And I'm going to stay in bed all day."

"Me? No, sir. I'm hardened. I could start out now and walk to the next camp. Just as soon as I drink this next cup of coffee."

"Then I won't see you again."

"Oh—sure." Hammond's mental processes were slow. "I was just kidding. What's your first name?"

"Miss Benson will do very well."

"Oh, I get you. High hat."

Claudia was satisfied. Jack Hammond left her alone after that. Later at the camp fire he pointedly avoided her. He sat with Douglas Kramer, who looked downcast and lonely across the leaping flames, for the radio singer with whom he had been flirting the greater part of the day had not stayed for the camp fire, but had gone off to her tent for the night immediately after dinner.

Beside her was Mr. Turley. She hadn't talked with him at all until after dinner when he asked if he might sit in the vacant chair next to hers. He asked if she objected to his pipe, and when she said her father had been a pipe smoker, and that she felt that pipe smokers were the salt of the earth, that sort of broke the ice between them.

Turley seemed a merry sort; at any rate, there was a sparkle in his dark eyes and the least sally of humor made him shake with mirth. He did too much punning, though. Naturally, she thought, he was a shy sort of man.

"Are you interested in ballads?" he asked.

"Yes. Are you?"

"I know some old California ballads. I'll sing some if I can find a guitar." He got up and went to inquire, but there wasn't any kind of musical instrument in camp. But he promised to sing at the next camp if there was a guitar or mandolin to be found there.

Only a handful of the party remained to enjoy the gathering around the fire. One by one they began to slip away. Miss Forbes and old Mr. Fulton found amusement in the fact that the younger members began to drift away first. They and Bruce Milbank and Professor Rogers wanted to tell stories. But Claudia's eyes, hypnotized at first by the firelight, became heavy-lidded. She found herself nodding, and then coming to with a start.

"Good-night," she said at last, getting up resolutely and starting away. "I guess I'm too young for this crowd."

Laughter followed after her as her heavy boots

crunched away in the rocky soil. The chill of high altitude was in the air. She passed the men's dormitory tent and came to her own, which was next beyond Miss Forbes'. Some of the women had gone together in the women's dormitory, but Claudia preferred to sleep alone. She shivered at the prospect of undressing in the cold. There was a small sheet-iron stove in the tent, but she could be in bed before it heated up. After all, one ought to get hardened. So she laid out her pajamas, then turned off her light and undressed and buried her shivering body under the pile of blankets. There was a light burning outside which threw solid black shadows upon the tent wall, but she was too tired to wonder whether it would keep her awake. But sleep did not come at once. Everything was so still. There was no place so quiet as the Sierras at night; the wind seldom blew.

It seemed hours later that she heard the last of the party walking by outside to their tents. She was too tired to do more than doze. Aching muscles roused her and she lay in dull wakefulness. The light had been turned out and darkness was complete; the silence was absolute. There was no stirring of air among the pines. She slept fitfully again. A noise awakened her. She lay wide-eyed in the cold listening. There were repeated small noises, furtive, sly sounds; there was the clatter of a pail, or perhaps a garbage can lid. With a sigh she turned over and tried to sleep. Probably a skunk, or some other night-prowling creature was abroad.

But sleep, sound sleep, still eluded her. Dreams now troubled her. They were horrible dreams in which she walked along a precipice. She stood poised at the edge of it, and was about to plunge into the depths. But without falling she seemed at the bottom of the abyss and crushed under tons of broken rock. Life was being squeezed out of her, and her own blood ran red upon the white granite surface spread like the top of a table for miles about her. There was the ooze and trickle of blood and the dying beat of a huge pulse.

Claudia wakened with a start. Somebody near by was talking. The words were scarcely more than whispers; they had no body to them. With a feeling of thankfulness she realized that daylight had come, for the tent canvas was gray overhead.

"Didn't anybody hear anything at all?"

The whispered words were distinct. Claudia listened intently. The answer to the question was too low for her to catch.

"It will be shocking to the rest of the hikers. Very shocking." The words this time were in a low voice. Footsteps crunched away.

Claudia lay quietly for a moment, then threw back the blankets and climbed out upon the cold wooden floor of the tent. She struck a match and dropped it into the little sheet iron stove where kindling and wood were already placed. The fire blazed up, and she dressed by its growing warmth. She tried to heat water to wash her face, but it was too slow, so scorning the softness of warm water, she poured from the pitcher into the white wash bowl on the battered washstand and scrubbed her face. All the while something urged her to get outside, to discover what had happened.

She untied the strings of the tent flap and stepped outside. Miss Forbes was walking by, neatly dressed in gray tweed skirt and green sweater. She heard Claudia coming and turned to greet her.

"You haven't heard, I suppose, about Mr. Hodges?"

"What happened?"

"They found him dead in his tent. He'd been——"

"Don't say it, please," begged Claudia horrified.

"They seem to think it was murder."

6

BRUCE MILBANK walked the short distance from camp to the ranger station. Huntoon Rogers accompanied him. Neither spoke as their heavy boots struck sharply in the rocky soil. The sun was just beginning to light up the somber junipers on the rocky ledges of the granite walls that hemmed in Merced Lake; the lake still lay in shadow.

Milbank rang the government center down on the Valley floor. The rangers at the station were eating breakfast. Rogers scanned a map on the wall. Milbank rang again.

"Get Mr. Plummer for me, please," he directed. "It's urgent. Milbank calling from Merced Lake."

"How soon can he make it up here?" Rogers asked, as Milbank waited impatiently.

"He'll get a saddle horse, of course. Middle of the morning, I'd say. Hello." He turned back to the telephone. "Mr. Plummer? . . . Bruce Milbank at Merced Lake—"

"What's happened? I was just getting up—" Plummer's voice was a trifle sharp in Milbank's ear.

"The worst that could happen, sir. One of my party is dead."

"Not old man Fulton?"

"A man named Hodges. Harry Hodges. We found him dead in his tent a few minutes ago—"

"Trip too much for him, eh? Heart, do you think?"

"No. Something else. Might be suicide. Probably something else. There's a chance that somebody killed him.

While he slept."

"Now, wait a minute, Bruce. Are you in your right mind?"

"Absolutely! Professor Rogers is here; he'll confirm—"

"It isn't that, Bruce. Sorry I spoke that way. But—what you're saying—I can't believe it yet."

"I'd like instructions, Mr. Plummer."

"This is Tuesday. You lay over all day there, of course. Well, I'm coming up, naturally, as soon as I can get there. Meantime—are you sure it's murder?"

"There's a good chance of it. Professor Rogers and I are agreed."

"All right. Preserve any evidence you may have, and don't let your party scatter; keep 'em together until I get up there. We'll have to hold some sort of investigation. Understood?

"Yes, sir."

"Good-bye. I'll get there as soon as possible."

Breakfast at the camp was a meal of strained silences, which were broken by brief bits of conversation. Hunger had brought the party together promptly, but news of the death of one of their number, now known to all, put no damper upon appetite. There were questions at first, all of which Milbank parried. It was true that Hodges had died in the night; it was true that the circumstances were mysterious, but nothing could be known until after the chief ranger arrived and made an examination.

"I want to say this, though," Milbank remarked, "in case any of you feel the need of exercise to work out the stiffness in your muscles—" several of the party interrupted with groans—"you are requested to do your exercising near camp where you will be within call."

"How about a little fishing while we're waiting, Mr. Milbank?"

"Fishing's all right, Mr. Stoner, if you don't get too far away."

"Has the sheriff been notified?" Jack Hammond inquired, setting down his coffee cup.

"The sheriff doesn't enter the picture, Mr. Hammond." Milbank's words were crisp. "The park is under federal jurisdiction. The ranger staff is charged with the duty of investigation and arrest of the guilty person. There is a resident United States commissioner in the park who holds the preliminary hearing and binds over to a federal court down below."

"So we're up against Uncle Sam himself in Yosemite."

"That's right."

"Now, listen, everybody." Hammond turned from Milbank to the others about him. "Don't get me wrong. I may have sounded like I know something about this that maybe I shouldn't. I'm not afraid of Uncle Sam, because I haven't done anything. That was just the way I speak out of turn sometimes. I was just interested in how they do things in Yosemite; that's why I asked about the sheriff."

The breakfast party broke up without comment from anyone. Outside, the DeWitts ambled off toward the lake. Claudia Benson, Miss Forbes, and Beryl Lindsay strolled away in close conversation. The others scattered about the camp. Milbank and Rogers sat on a bench together.

"I understand you're something of a detective, Mr. Rogers."

Rogers looked at the young man, a faint smile on his lips.

"Where did you hear that?"

"Superintendent Haverly told me you were interested in a matter that's been puzzling the park service. Understand," he hastened to add, "I haven't mentioned this to anybody else. I was advised not to. I was to make a place for you in the party if you cared to go with us, and if you wanted to offer any explanation of your presence that was up to you."

"Thanks. I appreciate that, but——" Rogers paused.

"But what?"

"Any reason why we can't look around before Plummer gets up here?"

"We can't do any harm. Not when it's you who are experienced."

They walked to the tent where the dead man lay. It stood in the shadow of a white fir. The pair had been there earlier, as had several of the men of the party when it was first discovered the man was dead.

"Not a pretty sight," said Milbank, wincing as he held open the tent flap for Rogers.

"Usually they're not."

They stood silently in the small space, their eyes searching minutely the still gloomy interior. The dead man's clothes were laid neatly upon a chair. His hat was hung on a corner of the mirror of the small dresser, the feather in the ribbon glowing brightly against the dark rough felt. His unrolled pack was on the dresser.

"Stab wound, wasn't it?" said Milbank as if he would reassure himself of the facts.

"Yes."

"But where's the knife?"

"That's what I'm wondering."

Rogers pulled back the blankets with which the dead man had been covered. There was a stain that spread over a large area of the pajama jacket.

"But where is it?" asked Milbank.

Rogers did not say anything for several moments. He drew the blanket over the body once more.

"Gone."

"Gone?" echoed the naturalist. "How could it be? But —was it there in the first place? I mean am I seeing things that are not so?"

"I saw the knife in the wound."

"So did I."

"Of course."

"Somebody must have been here, then, while we were over at the ranger station calling Mr. Plummer."

"Probably."

"Look here—" Milbank suddenly was deadly serious. "There was no certainty that it was murder at first. Anybody with courage could commit suicide like that. Just lie on his back and plunge the knife into his chest."

"True enough. But now the knife is gone. Hodges wouldn't be able to remove it. Not after he was stone cold. We found him like that. Cold and the knife in his chest."

"The murderer came back, then, for the knife."

"Yes."

"Is that why you wanted to leave it in the body?"

"Not necessarily. I wanted Plummer to see. Suicide or murder? It wasn't definite which. It's turned out murder apparently."

"What do you suggest we do?" Milbank suddenly realized that he was somewhat jumpy. "Is there any evidence we can get?"

"I took what there was earlier. His billfold. The watch is still on his wrist. There's nothing of importance in his pack, just the usual articles." Rogers turned again through the few things on the small dresser. "A man naturally goes very light on a hike like this. He has almost nothing with him. Better gather up everything though, Milbank. Clothes and all. I'll look around for anything we may have missed."

He opened the drawers of the small washstand and found them empty. He moved the stand out from its corner of the tent and looked behind it, then when Milbank had finished gathering the dead man's clothes into a bundle, he did likewise with the dresser. He went down on his knees and crawled under the iron bed and got up again empty-handed. He poked in a patch pocket in the tent wall and climbed upon a chair to examine a small wooden beam from which the light cord hung.

"Nothing?" Milbank asked.

"Not a thing."

"But what could have happened to the knife, Professor?"

"It will show up somewhere—probably."

"You don't think it would be destroyed—thrown into the lake, say, or hidden where it never could be found?"

"That's possible, Bruce. You don't mind if I call you that? We'll likely see more or less of each other from now on."

"No, of course not."

They left the tent, and Milbank tied the flap. The sun was just beginning to penetrate the dark shadow of the fir tree which had enveloped the tent. He picked up the bundle of dead man's clothing which he had rolled into the lavender bedspread.

"I don't suppose there's any need now of setting a watch over this—" He indicated the body in the tent.

"We have everything of value." Rogers was positive.

"I'll leave this bundle with Mrs. Hope—the caretaker's wife. She's the cook."

"Yes, I know."

They walked in silence to the kitchen door where Sally Hope, with a suppressed shudder when she learned what the bundle contained, permitted Milbank to put it down in a corner of her kitchen. Milbank exacted a promise of her to keep an eye on it. She was a rotund motherly person with flabby cheeks and shrewd eyes.

"Is Mr. Plummer coming up?" she demanded.

"Yes, Sally."

"I have to size up the crowd so as to know how much to cook."

Milbank hesitated. "You might count on an extra one or two besides Mr. Plummer. I imagine one or two of the boys will come up when he does with a pack outfit to take the body down below."

"Don't you worry; there'll be plenty to eat for everybody."

They went around to a bench in the sunshine and sat down to wait. The chief ranger couldn't be expected for a couple of hours yet. Rogers was thoughtful and made no effort at conversation. Milbank wondered what his companion had found to do in the time since he left the Valley floor; he wondered what luck, if any, he had had in the problem of the dead man—that other dead man whose body had been found in Lost Valley. Yosemite was certainly having a run of luck. None of the hiking party had talked with him yet about the hike, the major part of which still lay ahead. He hoped nobody would want to turn back. He believed they'd all be better off for finishing the hike. That's the advice he would give them, if anybody should inquire.

Old Mr. Fulton strolled near the bench. He saw Milbank and Rogers, altered his course and came up. They made a place for the old man between them. He was smoking a cigar which he had just lighted.

"Have one?" He offered his case, but neither accepted.

"How did you stand the trip yesterday, Mr. Fulton?" Milbank asked.

"You saw me come in right on your heels, didn't you? Almost stepped on them." He nudged Milbank with a sharp elbow.

"I certainly did. But how do you feel this morning?"

"Fit as a fiddle. That hardening up process I went through down in the Valley was just the thing for me. I —any news, Bruce? About our tragedy?"

The elderly man was inquiring partly for conversational purposes, but there was a note of curiosity in his voice too.

"I think the whole thing had better wait, Mr. Fulton, until Mr. Plummer gets up."

"Yes. I guess you're right about that." Fulton was silent. "I'm saving what I know about the affair until then."

Rogers looked questioningly at the old man, but said nothing. Milbank was silent too, declining to draw the speaker out.

"You don't suppose, gentlemen— No, I guess not."

"What were you going to say, Mr. Fulton?"

"Just a thought that crossed my mind, Bruce. But it's no good. I don't see the connection. I was thinking of the knife Kramer found on the trail yesterday."

"Knife?" Rogers echoed.

"Down in Lost Valley," Milbank explained. "One of the party kicked it out of the pine needles as he was walking off the trail. Turned it over to me and I put it in my pack— Wait a minute!"

Bruce Milbank's jaw sagged a trifle, then he leaped up and went striding away. He disappeared inside the main camp building, and the screen door slammed behind him.

"Fine young man," commented Mr. Fulton. "Very capable."

"That's true of all the men in the parks service; from top to bottom they're fine fellows."

The door slammed again and Milbank came out, striding back to the bench. He halted before Rogers.

"That knife is gone. I had it in my pack."

"Yes?"

"It's just struck me now that there was something familiar about the knife handle I saw—when we first looked at Hodges in his tent. What followed—I mean, having to call the chief ranger and all—sort of knocked everything about it out of my thoughts."

7

CHIEF RANGER FLOYD PLUMMER dropped the tent flap and shut out the sight of the dead man inside. He glanced away to the white granite cliffs through the pine trees. His manner was thoughtful.

"What do you think of it, Hunt?" he turned to Rogers.

"I don't like it."

"Neither do I."

"But who would do such a thing?" Milbank's voice was anxious. "Surely not anybody in the hiking party."

"Who else would, Bruce?" asked Plummer.

"Well—maybe some hiker on his own here in the back country."

"Apparently the motive was not robbery," Rogers pointed out. "Money and watch not touched."

"Somebody with a grudge who was waiting for him," Milbank expanded his idea. "Somebody who knew he was coming on this trip."

Plummer was silent. He looked at Rogers.

"It's possible," Rogers agreed. "But the only way to get at the facts, Floyd, is to do some prospecting. Among the hikers."

"Well, let's get busy, then." The chief ranger's voice was crisp. His tall, spare figure led the way to the group already gathered before the main camp building.

Conversation ceased when the trio drew up before the assembled party. All eyes turned expectantly to the chief ranger.

"I should explain myself, ladies and gentlemen," he began after a few moments. "I'm Floyd Plummer, chief ranger of Yosemite. I want to say how very sorry the park service is at this unfortunate occurrence. We of the service have a big job to do in the park. I'm not embarking upon a lecture, but just let me point out that when a half million or more human beings in a single year come to this recreation area, all the instincts and passions, the motivating springs of human action are not left at home. Accidents are, of course, common; homicide, on the other hand, extremely rare. I'm afraid that homicide is what we have to deal with.

"Now, then—you came for an outing here in Yosemite, and the park service earnestly desires that you enjoy it to the full. I don't want, therefore, to take up your time unnecessarily, but you understand, of course, that in an unusual situation like this the ranger staff requires your co-operation. I'll be as brief as possible. What I want is to get at the facts in the unfortunate death of Mr. Hodges. Who can give me any information that has any bearing upon the case?"

There was a silence broken only by the distant cries of a nutcracker down by the lake. Several members of the hiking party exchanged quick, inquiring glances. There was a slight scuffling of boots as Leon Mullins dropped to a squatting position on the ground and pulled his fawn-colored hat down upon his forehead.

"It might be interesting, Mr. Plummer," he began with a slight drawl, "to know that Hodges' name wasn't Hodges."

"Not Hodges!" Plummer was astonished.

"His name wasn't Hodges. Or wasn't until lately, any-how."

"I wish you'd be a little plainer, Mr.—"

"Mullins. Leon Mullins, sir."

"Can you explain?"

"Well, when I knew him about ten years ago, he went by the name of Harry Britain. Now, whether his real name was Britain or Hodges—or even something else, like Jones, or Smith—I couldn't tell you."

"That's odd." Plummer appeared puzzled. He turned to Rogers. "You were saying, Hunt, there was nothing in the billfold—"

"Not even a card, or a driver's license—"

"He never drove a car," interrupted Mullins. "He was afraid of them."

"Well—" Plummer ran a hand through his sandy, gray-ing hair, and replaced his stiff-brimmed hat—"whoever the man was—Britain or Hodges or Jones—he's dead. Just now we're more interested in how he came by his death than in his identity. That can be threshed out some-where else and later. Under the circumstances it has to be—this is Yosemite, not San Francisco.

"I suppose you know by now," he went on, "that the victim was killed by a stab wound. The knife has disap-peared. The murder occurred some time during the night. At just what hour it is impossible at present to say, for the body was cold when it was found. Who, by the way, first discovered that the man was dead?"

Plummer looked about the circle of faces all intent upon his own. A hand was raised by Beryl Lindsay as if she were a student in school. Milbank mentioned her name to Plummer.

"Yes, Miss Lindsay."

"Unfortunately I was, Mr. Plummer. I don't know how in the world I happen to be so unlucky. It was terrible. One of these little golden mantle ground squirrels was on the path and I tried to feed it a peanut I had in my bag, and it ran under Mr. Hodges' tent—under the floor, that is— and before I realized what I was doing, I had got down on my hands and knees and looked under the floor, but I couldn't see the squirrel. As I got up I happened to glance into the tent. I thought what in the world would Mr. Hodges say if he should happen to look out at that moment and see me looking into his tent. The tent flap was open a tiny crack, and I just unconsciously—you know how your eyes are, you see before you can really help seeing—and there he was! I realized instantly that something was terribly, terribly wrong. So I ran to Mr. Hope who was outside here and told him."

"Thank you, Miss Lindsay," said the chief ranger, hoping that that was the only information she had to divulge. "Did anybody else hear anything, or see anything suspicious?"

"I heard something. I don't know what time it was," offered Jack Hammond. "It sounded like a garbage can."

"I heard that noise too," said Claudia quickly, then wished she hadn't because it gave Hammond something else in common with her.

"Was there a skunk around last night, Homer?" inquired Plummer of the caretaker of the camp who leaned against a tree in the rear.

"Yes, sir, Mr. Plummer. He tipped the whole can over. Made noise enough to wake up everybody in camp. Scattered garbage all around. Had to clean it up. That's what I was doing when Miss Lindsay came running to tell me about this here fellow being dead. I rousted out Bruce, who was just about to get up anyway. And—that's how things got started around here this morning."

Bruce Milbank realized that things were moving slowly. He wondered if there was a short cut to more vital information. He remembered Mr. Fulton. In an aside he spoke to the chief ranger.

"Mr. Fulton," Plummer began slowly, "do you happen to know anything that might be vital to this investigation?"

The old man pulled his slouch hat farther down upon his forehead. Only his sharp nose struck by a shaft of sunlight was visible; the eyes seemed to lurk in the shadows of the hat brim.

"Just this, Floyd— I guess I can call you Floyd. I've known you long enough."

"Of course. Go ahead, Mr. Fulton."

"While the boys, meaning Bruce and the professor, had gone off somewhere to telephone—the news had got about the camp, of course—I came out of my tent, which was right next to Mr. Hodges'. I'd been dressed and out around, of course, before that, but I'd gone back to get my sweater. And I heard somebody over there. I mean in the tent where the body was. I came out and started up this way, and as I went by I could see through the flap that somebody was in there."

"Do you know who it was?"

"Well—if he won't speak up himself, I'll give his name. I'd have to under the circumstances."

There was a stir, and Leon Mullins shifted his weight, picked up a small pebble and flipped it with his thumb at a jay hopping stiff-legged along the ground.

"He means me, Mr. Plummer," said Mullins. "I went in to see Harry. Just to satisfy myself that he'd got it."

"You untied the strings and went inside the tent?"

"Yes, sir. When I went away I tied the flap again."

Plummer hesitated. He didn't know what had been uncovered by this admission. He consulted with Rogers. Rogers had a question.

"Will you tell us what you saw, Mr. Mullins?" he asked.

"You mean how he looked?"

"Just what you saw. The appearance of the body, and the general interior of the tent, say."

"Well, the knife was sticking in him. That was the one big thing. It was about the only thing I could see. As I said, I'd heard the news as soon as anybody else. All I had in mind was to make sure it was so; that Harry was dead; that he actually had been killed. When I satisfied myself about that, I came out. I didn't think anybody had seen me. I guess I was too taken with what I was seeing inside the tent to hear Mr. Fulton outside. It's a terrible experience to look on the body of a fellow human who's been slain in the night."

"Anything else?" prompted Rogers.

"That's all." Mullins pulled his hat tighter upon his head. "Unless you're figuring to ask me if I killed him. If you are, I'll answer that one before you ask it. I didn't. What's more, I don't know nobody who would do that."

"Thank you," said the chief ranger.

Rogers persisted. "Mr. Mullins, you stated that the knife was still in the body. Could you have been mistaken?"

"No, sir. That was the biggest thing in sight in the tent. My eyes just sort of froze to that knife."

"Had you ever seen the knife before?"

Mullins thought carefully. "Now that you mention it, Mr. Rogers, the handle looked something like the handle of that knife Mr. Kramer found yesterday in Lost Valley."

The information caused a stir among the hikers. Many eyes came to rest upon Kramer. Suddenly he burst out:

"Don't accuse me, anybody. I was dead to the world last night. Slept like a log till I heard the commotion outside the dormitory tent this morning. That's all I know. I gave the knife to Milbank."

Milbank moistened his lips. "That's right. I put the knife in my pack. I don't know when or how the person who killed Hodges got it from the pack. But the knife has disappeared now. Someone visited the body after Mr. Mullins was there, and removed it."

The chief ranger interrupted. "I hope," he said quietly, "that no one jumps to conclusions as to the identity of the guilty person. Let me point out that you start tomorrow on the next leg of your hike. I hope that you carry with you no unfounded suspicions of your companions. Mr. Milbank suggested to me earlier that perhaps some lone hiker in this back country, someone who harbored a grudge against the dead man, may have known of his plans to go on this trip, and lay in wait for him, so to speak. That is something to be investigated. For your peace of mind, we keep a check on all such persons in the high country, and will start at once to run down that angle.

"One or two more questions and I think I'll have troubled you enough," he went on. "Who had the tent on the other side of Mr. Hodges? You recall Mr. Fulton saying that he was on one side."

He waited for an answer which was slow in coming.

Finally from the rear of the group came a voice.

"I did, sir. My name's Frederick Dudley." The man had a quiet, deliberate way of speaking. His light gray eyes looked oddly out of place in his sunburned face.

"Thank you, Mr. Dudley. Tell me, please, whether or not you heard anything of a suspicious nature in the night at the tent where Mr. Hodges died?"

Dudley seemed to weigh his reply. "I may have." He was slow to amplify his remark. "There was a noise of some sort. I was dead tired. I'll sleep even better tonight."

"What sort of noise, please?"

"Oh, a noise. When something wakes you up and it's still dark, and you're sleepy, you're never sure what wakens you. If I'd been down at Camp Curry, I'd say it was the kind of noise a deer might make poking about the tents."

"Is that what it sounded like?"

"I think so. But I dropped off again without analyzing the sound, or even thinking about it. In another hour or so I probably would have forgotten that I heard anything at all."

"Thank you, Mr. Dudley. Anything else?"

"No, sir. That's all."

"Who slept where last night? Mr. Kramer mentioned that he was in the men's dormitory tent. Who else was with you, Mr. Kramer?"

Douglas Kramer thought a moment. "Professor Rogers, Mr. Turley, Jack Hammond, Mr. Mullins, Mr. Stoner, and Mr. Milbank."

"Hodges and I traded tents last night," said Thomas Fulton. "I can't sleep if the springs sag the least mite. He said he didn't mind, and so we changed."

"Who knew of the change?" Plummer's pulse quickened.

"Why, nobody, I guess, except Hodges and me."

"I knew about it," said Miss Lindsay. "I went by when you were making the change and asked you what you were doing."

"Yes, I remember now you did." Fulton leaned forward to look at the school teacher.

"Who else, now, can remember something worth noting?" asked Plummer.

"Mrs. DeWitt and I had a tent together. My name's Al DeWitt."

"Yes, Mr. DeWitt?"

"I don't know whether this is important or not. But when my wife and I came for breakfast, she was lagging behind as usual—" He dodged as if expecting a blow from his wife, who sat tight-lipped beside him. It was intended to be funny, but no one laughed. "And I looked back," he went on soberly. "If you'll notice you can see from here down the path to the tent where Hodges died. Well, just as I looked back there was some sort of movement down there. I didn't get it. Maybe I didn't see anything. But whether I did or not, all of a sudden a bird—one of those blue rascals—like that one over there—went squawking up from behind the Hodges tent into a tree. Raising hell. You know how they're always sticking their noses into whatever is going on, then flying off screeching bloody murder. That's all."

"And you think there was somebody down there?"

"Your guess is as good as mine."

"Had all the party gathered for breakfast up here?"

"Most all."

Ruth Sherman spoke for the first time. "There were only two places vacant at the table when the DeWitts came in," the radio singer announced.

"Yes?"

"Mr. Hammond's and Mr. Turley's."

"Now, listen, babe!" Hammond exploded in protest. "You're accusing me of killing a man. And I'm not in that racket. Besides, the guy was a perfect stranger to me."

"Mr. Turley?" the chief ranger prompted, ignoring Hammond. "What do you say for yourself?"

"I seem to have been the one person who didn't know what had happened; that is, until breakfast time. I overslept. As it was, I beat Mr. Hammond to the table by half a length."

William Turley's brown eyes twinkled as he looked from the perturbed Hammond to the chief ranger. He turned his attention to his pipe. The tip of his index finger was missing, and he tamped the tobacco in the bowl with the stub.

"And you don't have anything to add to what we know?"

"Mr. Plummer," the reply was emphatic, "if I had known anything at all I'd have been the first person to speak up."

8

IT WAS nearly noon when the final question was asked, and the hikers excused. From the trail along the lake two mounted rangers, one leading a pack mule, rode into camp. They halted as Plummer called out. Plummer and Rogers, accompanied by Milbank, walked over to them. Rogers was introduced.

"It's nearly noon, boys," Plummer said, consulting his watch. "Better eat first. Then I'd advise waiting till your dinner's settled. We'll tackle the job after that. There's no particular rush to get the body down below; it might be well if you didn't plan to reach the Valley floor until dark so as not to attract too much attention to what's on your pack mule."

The two rode away among the trees. Bruce Milbank looked at his chief and then to Rogers.

"Well, did we find out anything important?"

Plummer's eyelids narrowed; he looked away and then his gaze returned to Rogers. "What would you say, Hunt?"

"You never know, Floyd. You laid a foundation; and that's always necessary."

"Anybody lying to us?"

"Probably. You never get the unmixed truth at the first fishing for it."

"Then you think the killer is one of the hikers?"

"I wouldn't be dogmatic about it. Bruce's suggestion that some hiker on his own might have done it should

69

be checked."

"I'll put some of the boys on the job. Meantime, Hunt, have you any plans of your own?"

Rogers was thoughtful. "This other matter is at sort of a dead end—the Hugh Buckingham case."

"Figure to spend more time on it?"

Before Rogers could reply, Milbank recalled something of the afternoon before. "Hugh Buckingham?—the initials 'H.B.'— Those initials were on that knife we found yesterday."

"The knife that killed Hodges?" Plummer asked.

"I'm quite sure of it. They didn't mean anything to me at the time. I didn't know anything about any Hugh Buckingham."

"Queer," said Plummer, looking at Rogers. "Could be just a coincidence, don't you think?"

"It could be." Rogers was silent. "You know, Floyd, I believe I'll go along with the hikers tomorrow. Perhaps I'll go all the way with them. I certainly will go as far as Tuolumne Meadows."

"I'll feel better about it, Hunt, if you'll do that," Plummer said forcefully. "Not that Bruce isn't capable of handling the party. It isn't that. But if there's a chance the murderer is one of the hikers, the park service would appreciate your efforts to clear the thing up. I'll probably stay over here until I've made a satisfactory check."

"Naturally I'll do what I can," Rogers said. "This other case, though, is on my mind. I've got to do some thinking about it. That's why I came up here—knocking around on mountain trails sort of stimulates my thought processes."

"Suit yourself."

The call to the midday meal sounded and the hikers who had remained in the camp area reassembled in the dining room. Milbank was amused to note how both Claudia Benson and Ruth Sherman were at pains to avoid Hammond. Douglas Kramer had begun again his flirtation with the radio singer. Miss Forbes, he noted, had a way of pushing in at the top; she sat between Rogers and the chief ranger.

All this was encouraging to Milbank; in it were signs that the hikers were returning to normal. As soon as he could get them away from Merced Lake and on the trail once more everything would be all right again, and he could be credited with another successful hiking party. In spite of the tragic mark already on it.

He reached into his coat pocket for his handkerchief to wipe the perspiration from his face, for the coffee had heated him up. He wished he had left his coat off, for the sun by midmorning had warmed the air until a coat was uncomfortable, and he had taken his off and hung it on a stub of a pine tree.

He felt something unexpected on top of his handkerchief. It crumpled softly in his fingers and he identified it as a piece of paper. He drew it out casually, wondering what it was, and the less than a dozen words written on it seemed to rise up and strike him. They were written in pencil on the torn half leaf of a notebook. It required no second glance for him to know that he had never seen the handwriting before. With a quiet movement he slipped the note back into his pocket again, forgetting that perspiration still stood in tiny drops on his forehead.

Milbank glanced about the table to see if anyone had been observing him, but he saw no sign that anyone was interested in him at the moment, nor was anybody pointedly ignoring him. He wondered who had taken this means of communicating with him. His gaze rested swiftly in turn on every face he could see down the table, but he could arrive at nothing.

It was obvious, of course, that somebody during the time his coat hung on the tree had slipped the note into his pocket. Was it before, or after, the inquiry? Was it while he was talking with the boys who had come up for the body? For he had not taken the coat off the tree until just as he came in to lunch. Milbank was glad when the meal was over and he could get free of the party for a word with Plummer and Rogers alone. He pulled the note out of his pocket once more and handed it to his chief.

"Here is something I don't understand, Mr. Plummer," he said. "It was in my pocket. I discovered it during lunch."

The chief ranger read the brief words, and gave the slip of paper to Rogers.

"What do you make of this, Hunt?"

Rogers read it aloud: " 'One of the party washes his hands so frequently. Why?' "

"Can you figure it out, Professor?" asked Milbank.

A faint smile came and went on Rogers' tanned face. "We have a busybody in our midst, who would call our attention to something that may not be of any importance whatever."

"Afraid to accuse a fellow hiker," commented Plummer.

"But don't you think it could mean more than that, Professor?"

Rogers shrugged his shoulders. "It could, yes, Bruce. Maybe the writer of the message is more of a student of psychology than we give him credit for. And a keen observer."

"But if that were true—" persisted Milbank.

"Well—for lack of a better term perhaps the writer has observed what might be called a Lady Macbeth complex at work—'All the perfumes of Arabia will not sweeten this little hand,' " he quoted. "Keep your eyes open, Bruce. It's an interesting angle."

The matter was dropped there just as Beryl Lindsay came striding up. Her round plain face was good humored and expectant.

"Mr. Milbank, couldn't some of us get away for a little hike this afternoon? You won't be asking any more questions."

"Of course. As many as want to go. I'll take you on a hike to Washburn Lake. You'll enjoy it."

"Get your party going any time you like, Bruce," instructed Plummer. "There's no more investigation. And these people have asked to be shown the high country." He smiled at Miss Lindsay, who went away to spread the news.

It was not until the hikers had disappeared on the trail to Washburn Lake that the chief ranger and Rogers went around to the camp's kitchen. Sally Hope and her helper, a boy of nineteen, were finishing up the dishes.

"What can I do for you, Mr. Plummer?" The woman's manner was brisk.

"We want to talk to you. Can we come in?"

"If I were you I'd rather set outside on the bench. I'll come out. Go ahead and finish up, Wallace," she said to her helper.

The three sat down on the bench in the shade of a pine tree, and the plump, middle-aged woman looked inquiringly to Plummer.

"What do you know about the death of Hodges, Sally?"

"Exactly nothing, Mr. Plummer. What would I be expected to know?"

"You didn't hear any noise in the night? Nobody ran by your window breathing hard?"

"No noise except what the skunk made. I guess everybody in camp heard the racket when he tipped over the garbage can. These skunks around here are gettin' as bad as the bears used to be."

"Of course the crowd was all strange to you last night, but have you got any suspicions, Sally? A person might see something, or overhear something significant."

"No."

"Any hunches?" There was a suggestion in Plummer's manner that he found Sally Hope amusing.

"Don't have 'em. If I did I'd get rich playing the races."

"Have you seen anybody among the hikers washing his hands oftener than would ordinarily be necessary?"

Sally Hope gave the chief ranger a look which indicated she doubted his good sense.

"What a question! I don't keep track of how many times a guest washes his hands. I'm too busy."

"Yes, I suppose you are. Have you seen anything of a knife? Horn handle. Hunting knife. Probably about that long." Plummer measured with his index fingers.

"You mean the knife he was killed with—the gentleman?"

"Yes."

"If I had, I'd said something about it before now."

The screen door behind them opened on squeaking hinges.

"Did you say a hunting knife, sir?" asked a voice.

Wallace Rosen, a ruddy, curly-haired youth, stood in the doorway looking out at the trio on the bench.

"A hunting knife with a horn handle."

"Is it the knife the man was killed with?"

"Yes. What do you know about the murder?"

"Nothing, sir." The door squeaked shut, and the youth was about to disappear from view.

"Then why did you ask?"

The door opened again and the curly head was stuck out.

"I just thought I'd ask, sir. I saw a knife somewhere this morning when I cleaned up the tents and made the beds."

"What kind of knife, and where was it? Come out here where I can see you better."

The youth came out. "I don't think it could have been the knife you're looking for."

"Let me be the judge of that. Where is the knife?"

"Well, I don't know where it is now, sir. It's been a couple or three hours since I saw it. I didn't know how the man got killed. Nobody would tell me, and when you all were talking about it out in front, I had to be back here peeling potatoes."

"Let's go see if we can find it."

The chief ranger and Rogers got up from the bench.

"Is that all you want of me, Mr. Plummer?" asked Sally Hope.

"Yes, Sally. Thanks. Now, Wallace, take us to the knife."

The trio set off, the camp helper leading the way in a long loping stride among the tents now deserted by the hikers. The youth hesitated between two tents beyond where the body of the dead man lay.

"This was the one, I think." He pushed aside the flap and ducked inside. Rogers and Plummer crowded in beside him. "But it ain't here." The youth was somewhat taken aback.

"Are you sure this is the right tent?" demanded Plummer.

"Yes, sir. I remember that pack there on the dresser. Everything is new. I mean the pack things. And the knife was laying right behind the pack. Sort of hidden, but not so as you couldn't see it."

"Was the knife bloody?"

"No, sir."

"Did you pick it up and examine it?"

"Well—I'm not supposed to touch things, sir. Unless I have to move 'em to make up the beds and straighten around. But to tell the truth, knives interest me, and I picked up this one."

"Describe it."

"It was about so long, with a horn handle, and some initials were scratched in it."

"What were they?"

"They looked like an 'H' and a 'B,' sir. The 'B' could have been an 'R.' I don't remember exactly."

"Whose tent is this?"

Rogers answered the question. "A name is on the toilet set." He picked up the black leather case. "Frederick Dudley," he read.

9

CLAUDIA BENSON breathed deeply of the clean, cold air. There was a tang of pine forests in it. She was amazed at how fresh and eager she felt now that her muscles had limbered up once more. The day's hike was over the pass to Vogelsang camp. They'd climb almost to eleven thousand feet. The thought of what lay ahead filled her with anticipation. She knew she wouldn't get so tired today as she had on Monday. The short hike the day before from Merced Lake camp to Washburn Lake had taken the kinks out of her muscles, and she now felt capable of walking almost any distance.

"Do you think you'll make it?" asked a voice at her elbow. She glanced up to discover the tall figure of Frederick Dudley striding beside her. He had been so silent the first day, so compressed into himself that she'd not had a word with him. He smiled, and his light gray eyes set oddly in his heavily tanned face lighted up in a friendly way.

"I could walk there and back the way I feel now."

"You were pretty tired Monday when we got in."

She hadn't thought that he had noticed anything that first day. He hadn't really thawed out until dinner time the evening before, and later around the camp fire. He had had a lengthy conference with the chief ranger and Professor Rogers after the party got back from Washburn Lake. It had been heated at one time and Mr. Dudley seemed to be quite angry. He had pounded his right fist into the open palm of his left hand, and stamped his feet. That was after the park rangers had started down to the Valley floor with the body of the dead man. They had got Wallace Rosen, the camp helper, into the argument, and that was why dinner was ten minutes late. But that was all past now. She wanted to forget all the fright and unpleasantness she had experienced at the camp.

"Yes, I was tired that day."

Nothing more was said for some moments, then Dudley remarked: "They sort of had me over a barrel yesterday, the chief ranger and Mr. Rogers."

"What happened?"

"I was accused of having had the knife that killed Hodges in my possession after the murder."

"Really?" Claudia was startled.

"Don't you want to sit for a breather? We've been climbing pretty steadily. Besides we've got all day to hike less than ten miles."

They sat down on a granite boulder beside the trail. Those behind walked on past them.

"What happened?" Claudia was interested now.

"I denied it, naturally. It wasn't true. I didn't see the knife at any time, certainly not after it was used to kill Hodges. We all saw it, of course, when Kramer produced it in Lost Valley."

"How awful to be accused like that!"

"It was one of those curiously embarrassing things. Under questioning the boy became confused and admitted it might have been somebody else's tent where he saw it. He stuck to his guns, though, that he had seen the knife after it had been taken from the body."

"The whole thing is so horrible that I want to forget it."

"So do I. The only reason I mentioned it at all, Miss

Benson, was because you happened to walk by while I was being questioned, and you must have overheard some things that were being said. I wanted you to know that I cleared myself of suspicion."

Claudia was glad that he had explained it to her. They sat for a while longer and she learned that he was an architect in San Diego. He and his wife were separated. When he began to talk about that, Claudia got up and started on. Men were all alike. She might have known that it was his marital troubles and not the knife that he wanted her to know about.

"I think we'd better start on, Mr. Dudley," she said, looking forward along the trail. "We'll get behind the others." She knew, though, that Miss Forbes was just ahead of them sitting on a rock. She had seen her through the undergrowth.

Miss Forbes joined them. They took up the trail once more and the conversation got far afield on the subject of modern art, which Miss Forbes seemed to know a lot about. Claudia rather liked the way Miss Forbes had reacted to the tragedy at Merced Lake. She seemed very calm and clear-headed about it; never at a single time had she seemed frightened or even particularly disturbed at what had happened. Only once had she made any comment and then she said rather an odd thing. Claudia remembered her words:

"Well, perhaps the world will go along just as it did before Mr. Hodges shuffled off this mortal coil." Miss Forbes seemed rather detached, as if she was passing judgment on something of no great moment. Claudia thought there might be some explanation; it was as though something more could or ought to be said. But nothing had been forthcoming.

There was a constant shifting about among the hikers
that made for variety of companionship. Claudia was beginning to like some of the hikers. Old Mr. Fulton was
entertaining. Mr. Turley had a droll sense of humor, but
spoiled it with too many puns. Beryl Lindsay had been
talking furiously all morning with Ralph Stoner about
fishing and the superiority of channel catfish to anything
else. She last saw the pair on the bank of the little mountain stream which paralleled the trail, and he was trying
to teach her how to cast.

"The Vogelsang area was a great gathering ground
for glaciers in the ice age," said a familiar voice at her elbow. The very sound of it seemed to freeze something
inside of Claudia. "Numerous glacial cirques abound, offer-
ing striking evidence as to the birthplace of a glacier."
Claudia walked on without so much as admitting she heard
Douglas Kramer quoting from a guide book. "The frail
knife-edged peaks such as Vogelsang were always above
the highest limits reached by glacial ice." Still Claudia ignored the young man.

"Interesting, isn't it?" he said, putting away a small
pamphlet.

"The radio singer appears to be much neglected," said
Claudia icily. Her boots struck more sharply upon the
rocky trail; her blond head was lifted even higher than
she ordinarily carried it.

"Oh, that! Forget it. She's got another blister coming
on, and I'm not going to tape this one. Let Milbank do it.
Now, you—you're sensible, the best head on the best shoulders in the whole of Yosemite—and everything else that
goes with it."

Claudia ran furiously forward along the trail; anything

to escape from Doug Kramer. She brushed rudely past Jack Hammond, who was talking with Leon Mullins, overtook Bruce Milbank, who was taping the blistered heel for Ruth Sherman, and ran far in advance of the party until she thought she had outdistanced them all when she encountered Huntoon Rogers sauntering along looking up through the trees at the gray, rocky crags that overhung the trail.

"What's the hurry?" he said, stopping her. "You'll get winded."

"I just wanted to get ahead," said Claudia, breathing hard. "This altitude—does get you."

"You're above nine thousand feet."

"Professor Rogers, do you believe in dreams?" Claudia burst out.

"Well—it depends upon what you mean by believing in dreams. The whole story about dreams hinges on their interpretation. Why?"

Claudia regained her breath before going on, then she said: "I had such horrible dreams Monday night at Merced Lake. There were incredibly high white precipices down which I was about to fall. Then, without falling, I was at the bottom under tons of rock, and there was blood, acres of it. It was horrible. Too horrible, really."

"That was the night Hodges died," commented Rogers. "I remember once having horrible dreams, a perfectly dreadful night of them. Next morning I learned that a man in the apartment house next door had committed suicide. The mind is a sensitive receiver of outside impressions in the dream state. It's possible that Monday night your mind was attuned to Hodges' final conscious moments."

"How terrible! Do they know anything yet about who killed him?"

"Nothing definite. By the way, have you observed anyone who is overcareful with his hands? Washing them often?"

"No. Why?"

"Forget it, Claudia. Are you keeping notes of your hike?"

"I'm not writing down anything. I'm one of those curious persons who never takes a note. I didn't all through your classes. Miss Lindsay and one or two others, Mr. Dudley and Mrs. DeWitt, are always jotting down something in their notebooks."

"That's interesting. By the way, have you noticed that Mrs. DeWitt and Miss Forbes are not speaking. Seem to avoid each other."

"No, I hadn't."

"I was wondering why. And Mr. Fulton seems to shy away from both of them."

The party stopped for lunch beside a tiny mountain stream that chuckled among the rocks, and then it pushed on up to the pass. They were above timberline, and to Claudia they seemed like tiny ants making their laborious way along the roof of the world. Vast panoramas of jagged, lonely mountain peaks were spread about the horizon. They could look down into velvety depths of forest on all sides. The little irritations of the morning hike dropped from Claudia's shoulders as she looked upon the immense vistas. She was glad that she had come on this trip. What was San Francisco? What was a job in a law office, when you could have this?

Throughout the rest of the day, during what remained

of the day's hike and in the late afternoon and evening at Vogelsang camp, Claudia felt a sense of exaltation. In all her life she had never seen such a sunset. It was the stark beauty of distant snowy peaks touched first with rose which changed to cold blue against an even colder blue-black sky that thrilled her. It was like something in a fantastic dream world from which she would awaken to ordinary scenes she had known all her life down at lower levels.

"It makes one feel how unimportant human affairs are," said Miss Forbes when it was all over. She lighted a cigarette and tossed the match away. The camp helper came and set fire to the wood in the pit in the campfire circle, and they sat around it for warmth, bundled in their sweaters. There was no softness about them in the night. The trees in the timberline forest about the camp seemed to huddle in fear of the great areas of bare rock faces. The intimate world they had known down below seemed remote. Like the trees, they huddled together about the campfire as if for protection against the unknown forces surrounding them. No one mentioned the camp at Merced Lake; the death of Harry Hodges was in all their thoughts, but against such an overpowering background, no one had the temerity to speak of it.

The party lingered at the fire until the logs burned down to glowing embers. Mr. Turley had borrowed a guitar from the camp cook and astonished them all with a repertory of ballads which he sang well. After that the group sang some songs to his accompaniment. Claudia was reluctant to leave the comfort of fire and human companionship to go to bed in the sharp, cold air that had settled upon the camp with the blotting out of the daylight. She wasn't nearly as tired as on that first day, but she was sleepy.

When the break-up time came, she sought her tent in company with Miss Forbes, whose tent was next to hers. They said good-night, and Claudia in the shortest possible time was buried underneath her blankets. She dropped off to sleep when the drowsy warmth of her own body enveloped her. The last she remembered was the whispering of the wind that tugged at the corners of her tent and moved with a moaning sound through the stunted pines.

Claudia came wide awake from dreamless sleep. Her heart was pounding. Her eyes opened wide upon complete blackness. The wind had ceased worrying at the tent corner. There was no sound whatever. Maybe it was early morning, else why should there be so little sleep left in her? There was no clock with illuminated dial to tell her the time; that was in her apartment down in San Francisco.

Something stirred on the dresser, then was set down gently. Claudia thought it sounded as if her small jar of cold cream had been disturbed. A chill like that of an icy knife struck deep within her breast. Her heart stopped its pounding for an instant, then began again louder than ever. Other articles were now being moved cautiously about upon the dresser top. Claudia thought of things like pack rats; they moved things about, traded you something for what they carried off. She wished she had asked Bruce Milbank whether there were pack rats in the high country.

The wooden tent floor creaked as under a heavy weight. No pack rat could do that. With a terrifying sense of helplessness Claudia realized that somebody was in her tent. What did he want? Why the shuffling about, the moving of things on the dresser? She didn't have any money with her, except for a little change and two ten-dollar bills.

All the strength within her suddenly gathered in her throat. She could scream for help. At that moment a cold hand closed upon her mouth and the whispered word of warning came to her ears.

"Don't!"

For a long time there was no other sound, and Claudia lay in terror that the cold hand would slip down and encircle her throat. The whisper came again.

"Keep still. Or you'll get what he got."

Claudia tried to open her mouth. The movement of her lips was like a signal to the hand, and it was removed.

"What do you want?" Claudia whispered.

"Where is it?"

"What?"

"I want what you found in your pack."

"I don't know what you're talking about."

"I want that little piece of jade."

"Oh. It's in my breeches pocket."

The whisper ceased. There was a fumbling, and presently Claudia heard the garment softly drop upon the floor. The floor creaked again; she heard the rough canvas of the tent flap pushed aside, and then the whisper, more like that of the wind than that of the disembodied voice:

"Thanks, sister."

IO

BRUCE MILBANK hung up the receiver of the camp telephone at Vogelsang, and went outside where the hikers were impatient to start the day's hike. The hour was later than on the other mornings, because the distance to Tuolumne Meadows was short.

"Everybody set?" Milbank inquired. "Let's go."

The party started away, waving final good-byes to the camp cook and the caretaker who stood in the door of the central tent. Milbank felt elated over his telephone conversation with the chief ranger. Nothing had happened to mar the trip since they left Merced Lake. In careful language he had conveyed the fact that nothing of importance had developed in the death of Hodges.

"Well, Bruce," the chief ranger had told him, "so far so good. And I'm hoping nothing new happens on the unwanted side. Keep in touch with me. Phone from Tuolumne Meadows this evening. Good luck."

The party moved down the trail with a spirit and enthusiasm that was encouraging. This group would turn out as had all the others. Even Miss Benson seemed to be more tolerant this morning of Doug Kramer. He was walking with her in a little group of four or five. That hadn't happened before. Always before she was running away from him with her head in the air.

There had been some sort of a row in the night among the women. He hadn't got to the bottom of it yet. All he had heard so far was that Miss Benson had become frightened in the night, had gone into Miss Forbes' tent where there was an extra bed, and had spent the remainder of the night there. Milbank wondered if it were bears. The camp cook had told him that there had been bears around a day or two before, but that the helper had run them off. They might have come snuffing about the tents in the night, but he had heard nothing himself in the dormitory tent where he had slept with the other men.

The party made its way down the slope to Rafferty Creek before anything occurred. The Oklahoma school teacher overtook him as he was walking at the head of the party with Huntoon Rogers. Her broad, beaming face was thrust between them and she began in her enthusiastic manner:

"Mr. Milbank, have I been seeing things?"

"I don't know. Have you?"

"Would you believe it, I saw a humming bird back on the trail just now! A humming bird! I just can't believe that those tiny creatures would be up here. Why, it's fully nine thousand feet."

"That's right." Milbank never knew whether to be amused or slightly irritated with Beryl Lindsay. But he had to take them as they came; that was part of his job. "Humming birds, sparrows— I've seen lots of small birds in Yosemite even higher than this."

"I'm going to make a note of it." She pulled a small notebook from the pocket of her faded jeans and fished out a stub pencil. She flipped through the leaves of the notebook, hunting an empty page as she walked along. "Now, how did that get torn out?" She stopped abruptly on the trail, her heavy boots striking fire on the rocky path. Milbank halted as did Rogers and they gazed at the notebook from which a leaf obviously had been torn. "Why, I bought it brand new down at Camp Curry, and I know I haven't torn anything out myself."

"Have you left your notebook lying around anywhere?" asked Milbank, recalling the note he had found in his pocket.

"I never leave it anywhere. I carry it right in my pocket."

"Are you sure?" Rogers inquired.

"Yes— No. Wait a minute. I'll have to take that back. I remember when Mr. Plummer was questioning us about Mr. Hodges. I took some notes of the testimony. Oh, nothing escapes me, boys. I put it all down—" she smiled broadly at them.

"And you parted with the notebook then?" Milbank pressed.

"I left it on the bench. Forgot it. It's funny how you remember things. Before that Mr. Mullins had been jollying me about writing down everything. And later, I mean after the investigation, I saw Mr. Mullins wiping his hands. It was the second time within an hour he'd done that, and it reminded me of his joking about my notebook, and I felt in my pocket and it wasn't there. Now, that's the only time it's been out of my possession. Somebody picked it up and tore out a page. You'd think they wouldn't—"

"You say Mr. Mullins was washing his hands—" interrupted Rogers.

"He seems an awfully nice fellow, but very quiet. I've had several long talks with him, though. He's very fastidious. Twice yesterday I saw him wash his hands in that little creek we followed almost up to Vogelsang Pass."

They let Beryl Lindsay talk on for a while, and then left her sitting beside the trail making note of the fact that humming birds were found at high altitudes.

Neither Rogers nor Milbank said anything as they walked onward together. For a time they were joined by old man Fulton, who like a young boy was chortling with glee that he had outdistanced the other hikers and was now taking the lead. The DeWitts closed up and walked with them, and finally when they were alone once more Milbank could not help the question:

"Is it Mullins who has the Lady Macbeth complex, Professor?"

"He seems a likely candidate."

The first stop for rest found the party in the upper reaches of the canyon through which Rafferty Creek flowed. Miss Forbes, who had been walking leisurely at the end of the line, striking at tree trunks and rocks with her stick, overtook the scattered hikers resting along the stream bank and continued until she found Milbank and Rogers seated on a fallen log. Her bright brown eyes came to rest upon them and she halted.

"If we can have a few minutes together, there's something I want to say," she remarked as she made herself comfortable.

"Go ahead," urged Milbank.

"It's about Harry Hodges."

"Yes."

"Well, I met him in Chile six or seven years ago." Miss Forbes poked at a stone with the tip of her stick. "He was running a sort of tourist agency, or guide service. He fixed up a trip or two for me into the mountains. But after I had spent a lot of money with him, I discovered he wasn't doing anything for me I couldn't do for myself and at much less expense."

"That's interesting," commented Rogers.

"You haven't heard anything yet. The only reason I'm telling you all this now is because I've been thinking it over ever since Hodges died, and however it may hurt somebody else I don't want to stand in the path of justice. It isn't right to keep still. But whatever happens I want you to know I'll go all out for Leon Mullins. It's Leon I'm talking about."

"Just how does he come into the picture?" Milbank asked.

"Well, I must tell you. Leon was the guide working for Hodges in Chile. He took me on a pack trip up into the Andes; and if ever I met a gentleman in a situation in which an unscrupulous man might have taken advantage of a gal like me, it was Leon Mullins. This was several years ago, mind you, when I was younger, more innocent and better looking."

"He's been a cowboy, hasn't he?" Milbank inquired.

"All his life, practically. Except for a brief tour of the dude ranch circuit where he got tangled up with Hodges. Hodges sold him on the possibilities of getting rich in South America off just such traveling suckers as I was. Hodges didn't have any money. Leon saved his, and that's the way the partnership got started. They'd been going for a couple of years when I happened to show up with an urge to see certain parts of Chile from the back of a mule. There'd been others before me, but probably not many, for things were going badly for them."

"Hodges was the brains and Mullins the brawn?" Rogers suggested.

"Exactly. Well," Miss Forbes continued incisively, "I

didn't fall for their extended tour of the country, which Hodges tried to sell me after I got back from the mule trip with Leon. Instead, I went my way on my own, and much cheaper. I went over the Andes and down into Argentina, and finally up to Brazil. It was on the boat from Rio to New York that I ran into Leon Mullins again. He remembered me, of course, for it was only a couple of months since I'd seen him. And did he have a story!"

"Tell us," Milbank urged gently.

"He and Hodges had busted up. Or, rather, Hodges had skipped out, taking the community funds, and leaving Leon flat. But listen, now. Leon had married a girl much younger than himself just before he went to South America. Took her down there. Maybe they weren't suited, maybe they would have got along all right if it hadn't been for Hodges who, it seems, would work on the girl's susceptibilities when Leon was away conducting tourist parties. Anyway, the upshot was that Hodges not only ran away with Leon's money, but with Leon's wife.

"Leon told me all this one night on shipboard. He couldn't help it; he just had to tell somebody. He'd tried to find Hodges and the girl; he'd traced them as far as Buenos Aires and lost them. He'd managed to earn passage money and was on his way home. But he kept saying over and over to me, 'If I ever get my hands on that'—you fill in the blankety-blanks—'If I ever catch up with him, I'll—' He kept saying it over and over."

She breathed a sigh and dug the tip of her stick into the rocky soil. "There, boys, is my story. But remember what I said, no matter what happens to Leon he's a gentleman, if not a scholar, and I'll go all out for him. I think I'll remind him who I am, and tell him what I've done in telling you."

"One more thing," Milbank said, as Miss Forbes got up.

"Yes?"

"What was the row about last night among the women?"

"Row? There wasn't any row. Oh, you mean Miss Benson. Well, she came over and stayed the latter part of the night in my tent. Something had frightened her and she didn't want to stay alone."

"I'm interested in what frightened her."

"She said somebody had been in her tent."

Neither of the two men spoke for a moment, and Miss Forbes regarded them critically as the information sank in.

"But that's not possible!" exclaimed Milbank.

"She was badly frightened. Came off just in her pajamas. Forgot her clothes. I had to go over early this morning and get them. Somebody—whoever it was—robbed her of something she had."

"Why didn't she say so?" Milbank was nettled. The blood slowly reddened his cheeks. "Why not tell us what's going on in this party? There wasn't any violence—?"

"Only that the person threatened to kill her if she screamed. Put his hand over her mouth so she couldn't."

"That's an outrage!" Milbank stood up, his lips thinned.

"I agree with you. Whether or not it's got anything to do with what's already happened, I'm not the one to say."

"I'm going to find out."

Rogers put out a restraining hand. "Just a minute, Bruce. Maybe Claudia Benson has a reason why she doesn't want to tell what happened last night. Don't you think we might give her a little more time to speak of it herself?"

"I might add this," Miss Forbes said matter-of-factly; "after she told me all this—which was in the middle of the night, mind you—Miss Benson thought better of it, and this morning after breakfast asked me not to say anything about it. She said she'd been having horrible dreams on this hike, and that she must have dreamed it. She didn't want to stir up any excitement and then be made ridiculous when it was proved that she'd only had a nightmare."

"She wasn't kidding you, was she?" Milbank eyed Miss Forbes.

"I don't think so. She was too earnest this morning, and quite apologetic for having broken in on me in the night."

"But she would know whether or not she had been robbed of anything," Milbank pointed out. "She could be sure that it was fact and not a dream that way."

"Yes, I suppose she could."

"Well, I'll give her a few hours longer to think it over before I say anything to her," Milbank announced.

Rogers got to his feet and stretched his arms over his head.

"Would you mind, Bruce, not saying anything to her at all at the end of a few hours, as you suggest. And let me take over the problem of Claudia Benson?"

"All right." Milbank was abrupt. He didn't know just what Huntoon Rogers meant, but there was some sort of hook-up between the professor and Superintendent Haverly, and he didn't want to trespass. "I think we'd better be moving on."

"And another thing," Rogers suggested. "For the present shall the three of us say nothing to the others of anything we've discussed here?"

"I'm mum," asserted Miss Forbes. "Maybe I've talked out of turn. I make it a rule never to repeat a mistake."

II

AT NOON the hikers dawdled over their lunch boxes. They had seemed in no hurry whatever since leaving camp at Vogelsang. Claudia had observed how the hikers frequently dropped beside the trail in twos and threes to talk. She had participated in several discussions herself. Bruce Milbank hardly had been able at any one time to get enough of the party together to point out objects of special interest. Beryl Lindsay was the only one he could count on. Ralph Stoner had gone back to Vogelsang after a few minutes away from camp. Somebody had told him the fishing was better down the Lyell Fork of the Tuolumne.

"I could tell you something about Miss Sherman," began Doug Kramer with brisk enthusiasm, as Claudia walked along hoping to be alone for a while.

"Not interested."

"Or I could tell you about the reddish mountains of this area. The region is very interesting geologically. The rocks are altered sediments and volcanics—remnants of similar material that once covered this entire area thousands of feet in depth."

"I read all that in the pamphlet too."

"I could tell you something else. About me. I'm delightful company on a hike like this. Helpful. Entertaining. Companionable. I'm a rising young lawyer who loves the nicest girl in the world. I'm ambitious. Right now my greatest ambition is to give back a ring to the nicest girl in the world. Said ring thrown at me in the snow over at Badger Pass last winter. You can't read all this in the pamphlet—"

"Why don't you let me alone?"

"Have you heard about the DeWitts?"

"No."

"He's getting scared."

Claudia did not reply.

"Charley horses, he says. He's just thought about them. They run in his family. Has a long personal history himself. Now he's worrying for fear he'll have an attack, or something. It could be something else, like losing his nerve."

Claudia walked on without making any reply. She felt sure Doug would tire soon of his effort to break down her resolution, and go elsewhere.

"Some of the fellows are talking of making book on Hodges. You know, Hodges, the fellow who died back at Merced Lake. Turley last night in the men's dormitory tent offered two to one that it was suicide. You're going to ask how about the knife I found. And what became of it. Well, that's Hodges' secret which he carried to his grave—"

"Douglas Kramer! Please let me alone. I don't want to hear any more of your ghastly humor."

"Sorry. I'll tell old man Fulton that you'd rather talk with him than with me."

Claudia walked on alone. She didn't understand why such persons as Doug Kramer had to be inflicted upon her. She'd rather be left to her own troubled thoughts than to be tormented by him. She wished heartily that a lot had not happened; if only she hadn't run in upon Miss Forbes in the night. That had been a mistake. She was going to quit sleeping alone. She was going into the women's dormitory tent with Beryl Lindsay and the radio singer at Tuolumne Meadows.

Up until last night she had thought highly of Maribel Forbes, but now she didn't know. It wasn't anything she could put her finger on. Until last night she hadn't realized how skilfully the woman could probe into things that did not concern her, how adroitly she maneuvered for information about other members of the party. She had been very curious about Professor Rogers. Who was he? Why did he seem to know so much that went on? Why did the chief ranger consult with him at Merced Lake? She had scores of questions expressed and implied, and Claudia finally had shut up like a clam. She didn't tell her about the professor's hobby; she hadn't told anybody about it. If there was anything Claudia disliked it was gossip about other peoples' private affairs. She had had to listen to too much of it in the past. But at least she didn't talk about others herself.

Footsteps crunched upon the rocky soil in her wake as someone came up from behind and was about to overtake her. She stepped aside to let the hiker pass, but instead the person halted. She looked up at the shrewd, small eyes in the lined face of Thomas Fulton.

"You look pretty solemn for a young girl," the old man said.

"I was just thinking."

"A young man told me that you had something to tell me."

Claudia's irritation at Doug Kramer's effrontery mounted. She concealed it, however, from the old man.

"I wish he hadn't caused you so much trouble, Mr.

Fulton. It wasn't anything. Just that you're a marvel. You strike me as the youngest person in the whole party."

"And isn't that something? That a man who will be eighty-one on his next birthday can outhike you young folks?"

The old man laughed, showing a mouthful of crooked, yellowing teeth. He sat down on a boulder, scooped up a handful of pebbles and tossed them, one by one, as he talked, into the brawling stream.

"How do you do it?" Claudia leaned against the trunk of a tree across the trail from him.

Before Mr. Fulton could reply, Al DeWitt and his wife passed between them with apologies. The man's face had lines of strain upon it, and yet he was scarcely more than half the age of the elderly man.

"There's the answer, young lady," he replied, nodding his head at the couple. "That man is henpecked. She's been pestering him from the moment we started, because it's her nature to do it. She's been telling him he'll never make it, sapping his self-confidence, gnawing away at his spirit. That's the beginning of DeWitt's downfall on this trip. Of any man's downfall. The spirit weakens first then the physical man weakens and fails."

"You're a philosopher, Mr. Fulton." Claudia laughed.

"No, I'm just experienced. I've lived a long time. At fifty-five, though, I was a wreck. Why? I had a domestic situation that would kill a dozen men. It nearly got me down. Nag, nag all the time. First one wife and then the other. Every nerve in my body was jangling like a thousand telephone bells all ringing at once."

"That must have been awful."

"It was. I kicked loose from it all, though. Got to the

point where I couldn't stand it any longer. Paid 'em all off. Wives and kids both. Told 'em to go their way and I'd go mine. And I've had peace and health ever since. I live here in Yosemite. Permanent resident. Did you know that?"

"No."

"Yes, I live the year round at the Ahwahnee."

"How fortunate you are."

"I live an ideal life for my age. I've forgotten the outside world. I've abandoned it to bubble in its own hell broth. My years, of course, are numbered, so why bother myself with social and political trends, with isms and cults that I'll never have to live with, because I have no future?"

Claudia was interested; she wished she had talked with the old man before now. To her he suddenly was the most entertaining person in the whole party.

"But what do you find to do?"

"Do? Plenty. I'm reading all the things I missed in my youth, and rereading all the things I enjoyed as a young man in college. I have a whole library of books. I'm going back to Tennyson, to Matthew Arnold, and Browning, and Dickens and Thackeray. To Goethe and Schiller and Shakespeare, to name only a few. I have a good phonograph and records of the music I loved and sang years ago. None of this ugly modern stuff. We used to be able to sing and whistle our songs when we were your age, young lady. You can't do that with the songs your generation is writing."

"The radio must be a great pleasure—"

"Radio?" The old man's voice rose to a squeak. "I wouldn't have one. I told you I've said good-bye to the world of today."

"Sorry."

"Do you think I'm crazy?"

"No. Everybody dreams of doing exactly what he pleases."

"That's what I'm doing," the old man chuckled.

"But few of us can afford it. We have to work."

"Do you have to work?"

"I love eating. No work, no eat."

"Mr. Haverly, the superintendent of Yosemite, tells me I'm crazy; that I'll go to seed living in the past. But I tell him I know what I'm doing. I came up here where the hills are eternal, and I've brought along the things that are eternal in my life. I've run out the hell cats and hell hounds that led me a dog's life. Told 'em all to go to hell, as far as I was concerned. I was through supporting them in idleness; they'd never get another cent of my money, then or ever."

Claudia didn't know what to say, and so remained silent. The old man's eyes glittered with tiny fires as he recalled his past.

"Do you know," he said, looking up at her oddly, "they've pretty well left me alone too. I don't know how they're making out, though. They never knew how to run their own lives, how to hold on to money when they were around me. What's more, I don't care very much. Except maybe for one or two of them we're through, quits, washed up, as they say. What do you do, Miss Benson? You've never told me. Have a pleasant home life?"

"If you call living in a tiny apartment, and not having any relatives, and having to work in a law office every day a happy life, then I have it."

"No young men?"

"None that interests me."

"There's a mighty likable young fellow in this crowd—named Kramer. Smart fellow. Lawyer. A good one too."

"He bores me."

Claudia was amazed at the frankness with which she was talking. Ordinarily she kept her troubles to herself, but somehow the great age of the old man sitting on the boulder tossing pebbles into the mountain stream was reassuring; he seemed like a valued counselor, and she was enjoying the talk with him.

"I'll tell him," was the amazing response, although she could see a twinkle in the shrewd old eyes.

"I wish you would. But it won't do any good. He's hopeless."

"Maybe it will, coming from me."

"You don't know Doug Kramer. He's my boss at the office."

"This is a queer crowd of folks. Now, that school teacher. Maybe she'd look all right in a dress, but her bulk in skin tight jeans—never."

Claudia was amused. "Don't you think too many women have grown careless with their dress in the last few years?"

"Yes. The old saying that clothes make the man was never truer, and it goes double for women."

"I thought you'd retired from the world," Claudia teased.

"One can't help seeing the world go by, even in Yosemite."

"Miss Forbes is the only one of the women in this party who dresses to please you, I suppose. She disdains slacks—"

"She always was a proper dresser."

"Oh, you've known her before?"

The old man apparently did not hear the question. Suddenly a strange little chill tingled at the back of Claudia's neck. She looked into eyes that seemed to be cold and bleak as the sharp, snowy mountain peaks that soared around them into the hard blue sky. An apology rushed to Claudia's tongue and then the silence between them became awkward.

"This Hodges fellow who died down at Merced Lake," began the old man. "Did you know anything about him, Miss Benson?"

"Only what was brought out at the investigation."

"Never heard anything about him from the others?"

"No, sir."

"Seemed like a well-meaning fellow. You wonder sometimes if it wasn't all a mistake. What had he done? Now, mind you, he wasn't the kind of a fellow I'd care to have around me. I always fired a fellow like him in my business organization. Sort of patronized me that first day coming up from Happy Isles. Called me uncle and wanted to help me up steep places. I had to tell him to go to hell once. He was sort of fuzzy-minded; didn't have a clear cut idea in his head. But things like that aren't enough to kill anybody for. You've talked with the others quite a lot, I've noticed. Nobody ever said anything about him? Where he came from, or anything?"

"No, sir."

"Funny that nobody knew anything about him. I suppose that among the rest of us, if we got killed off, nobody would know anything about us either. You for instance."

"Me?" Claudia was startled that he should turn it

on her like that. "Oh, but they would. Professor Rogers knows me. Douglas Kramer knows me. It isn't that I'd turn out to be Jane Doe number 324 and be buried in the potter's field."

A brief cold smile flickered in the thin face. "I've enjoyed this talk, Miss Benson. You seem a sensible sort of a girl, a level head on your shoulders. That used to be a compliment when I was younger. I never know, though, about this sophisticated generation of yours whether I'm being stuffy or not."

"Thank you. I'll accept it as you intend it, as a compliment."

The old man got up from his seat and looked back along the empty, winding trail. "I guess the others have all passed us."

"Yes, I'm sure of it."

"I'd like to ask a favor of you, if you'll be so kind as to humor an old fellow like me."

"I'd be glad to do you a favor."

"And not ask any questions, or tell anybody else about it?"

"Yes," Claudia said wonderingly. "What is it?"

The old man reached into his pocket, and drew out something which he held tightly in his fist. He seized her hand with somewhat of an air of furtiveness, of immense secrecy, and deposited the object in her palm, and closed her fingers over it tightly.

"Keep it for me. Don't tell anybody that you have it. Least of all that I gave it to you."

He turned from her and went striding forward along the trail.

A strange dryness was in Claudia's throat; a chilly hand seemed clutching at her heart. She knew what it was without looking. But even so she opened her hand and there lay the little green jade monkey.

12

CHIEF RANGER FLOYD PLUMMER's car pulled away from the camp at Tuolumne Meadows and turned into the Tioga Road. Huntoon Rogers settled deeply in the seat beside him with the air of a weary man welcoming the opportunity to rest. The car passed the store and the gasoline pumps, and the chief ranger acknowledged the greeting of a ranger standing in the tiny stone ranger station on the highway before anything was said between them.

"We'll get down to the Valley floor a little after sunset, Hunt," Plummer remarked.

"You say they found a registration of this fellow Wilkins, or Wilson at the Ahwahnee?"

"Yes. The Curry people put a girl on the job, and she's worked hard. It's no small job to run through six or eight months of records at the various camps and lodges."

"I appreciate that."

Plummer was driving down to the Valley floor in a much better frame of mind than he had driven up only a few hours before. The hiking party had arrived safely at Tuolumne Meadows. Nothing unusual had happened to it since the death of Harry Hodges. Bruce Milbank could have told him as much by telephone, but the chief ranger had wanted to make sure for himself, and had been on hand by the middle of the afternoon when the party came straggling in off the Vogelsang trail. Superintendent Haverly had been worrying about old Thomas Fulton, and had charged the chief ranger particularly before he left the government center to inquire. But the old man was looking fit and seemed to have more enthusiasm than the others at the end of the day's hike.

"I think it's important," Rogers interrupted the chief ranger's thoughts. "The registration at the hotel. Otherwise I'd stay at Tuolumne Meadows—"

"This fellow you were telling me about, who's washing his hands—"

"Leon Mullins."

"Mullins, yes. Is he still doing it?"

"We weren't able to check on him after Miss Lindsay pointed him out as the man. The thing fits in, though, with what Miss Forbes told Bruce and me this morning. It sets up an excellent motive for him. I was hoping that you might show up here and we could confront him with the information, but as I say, I think this other business is more important. Mullins can't get away. He can wait."

"Mullins is the best bet for the guilty man, is he?"

"At present."

They settled down to the long drive over the winding Tioga Road. Lush mountain meadows opened out in virgin forest, then were closed in again. Long vistas of dark timber and distant peaks came and went as the road wound through the heart of Yosemite; wildflowers covered the shoulders of the highway and stretched into the sunny areas among the trees. An occasional deer looked up from its browsing; a fox trotted across the road. Farther on a bear slept in the branches of a tree.

They traversed the old pavement and came to the new. The car slowed down at Crane Flat. Plummer waved to the rangers at the checking station but did not stop, and the car entered Big Oak Flat Road which descended in sweeping curves to the Valley floor. The sun was gone and the canyons were in shadow. The temperature increased as they dropped to lower levels. When they emerged from the last of the tunnels and came out upon the Valley floor, darkness had fallen.

"I think we'd better eat first," suggested Plummer as they approached Yosemite Lodge. "I'm hungry. The cafeteria is a good place."

"All right."

They parked and entered the still crowded cafeteria, selected their dishes and took them out upon the screened porch.

"I never cease marveling at the crowds here in the Valley," said Rogers. "So close to the empty wilderness of the high country."

"That's what worries Mr. Haverly," Plummer replied. "The great majority seek entertainment rather than recreation. As you and I understand the word."

"This registration was at the hotel, though," said Rogers. "Why not at one of the camps?"

"That's your puzzle, Hunt. If they'd started with the hotel records, the registration would have been turned up several days ago. But if you're doubting the registration, don't. I'll show you."

They paid their checks and drove the short distance from the Lodge to the government center. Rogers followed Plummer through the wide door of the administration building and down the short hallway to the chief ranger's office.

"There you are," said Plummer, and he drew from the drawer of his desk a registration card clipped to a typed memorandum. He laid beside it the register which had been brought down from Trumbull Peak.

Under the desk light Rogers compared the two signatures. At length he looked up at Plummer who awaited his reaction.

"I'm not a handwriting expert, Floyd," he said, "but I'm satisfied that the two are the same."

"There's no question of it."

"The date is different. They have it on the card February second. The fire lookout register says September seventh. He must have been here on two different occasions."

"Looks like it."

"The hotel people have interpreted the name as Wilsie, I notice. They've spelled it out here in the margin. So that's the name he was using."

"I hope, Hunt, that before you get through with this you'll tell us what it's all about." Plummer's voice was hopeful.

"I'm sure I shall. Now, I want to talk to somebody at the hotel. Somebody who can tell me about the man. I note he was at the hotel several weeks," he said, consulting the typed slip attached to the registration card.

"Let's go."

They went outside, climbed into the car and drove along the unlighted road to the hotel concealed under the dark shadow of North Dome. They parked and walked into the wide, high-ceilinged lobby and to the desk where Plummer asked for the manager. A plump youngish man soon appeared outside the desk.

"Hello, Mr. Plummer." He extended a cordial hand.

"I want you to meet Huntoon Rogers—Mr. Alderson, Hunt."

Alderson's heavy eyebrows lifted slightly. "Professor Rogers?"

"Yes."

"I'm glad to meet you. But I hope you're not moving in on us in a professional capacity, sir."

Rogers grinned. "I hope not too. May we talk with you?"

"Of course. Come this way." He led the pair into his office, pointed to comfortable chairs, and sat down at his desk. "Now what can I do for you?"

Rogers laid the registration card on the desk blotter, and Alderson glanced at it.

"Oh, that fellow. We're interested in him ourselves. He was a model guest, paid promptly, made no complaints of the service, got no mail. But he disappeared all of a sudden, owing us a two-day bill. We never got any trace of him, although we made inquiries."

"What about his baggage?" Rogers' eyes were eager.

"Just an empty suitcase in his room."

"Empty?"

"Absolutely. Must have carried away whatever he owned on his back. And that reminds me, he got a pair of snowshoes through the service and—we'd like those back too, or pay for them."

The chief ranger spoke up. "Those probably are the snowshoes we've got over at government center, Alderson. Found them in Lost Valley."

"With that body you can't identify?" Alderson asked.

"Yes."

"I'll send a man over tomorrow to check on them."

"All right. They're in my office. Found them only last week."

Rogers was impatient to get on with his questions. "How about identifying Wilsie's picture?" He pulled some photographs from his pocket.

"I can't do that," Alderson answered. "I don't remember the fellow. In fact, I never saw him. I came here a month or so after he skipped out. I rather think you might get more information from the maid on that floor." He picked up the receiver from his telephone set. "Get hold of Bertha. Tell her to come over right away." He returned the receiver to its cradle and sat back. "The maid will be over in a few minutes."

"I hate to bother her."

"She won't mind. Not Bertha." Alderson regarded Rogers critically. "I hear you had a little trouble up at Merced Lake Monday night."

"Yes."

"Does this—" he picked up the card and looked at it. "This fellow Wilsie have anything to do with it?"

"I would recognize Wilsie from his photograph. And Wilsie isn't in the party."

"Settles that point then." Alderson was interested. "Do you think it's somebody in the hiking party?"

Plummer answered. "It has to be, Alderson. We've been checking around ever since the murder occurred, on the theory that it might be somebody on his own in the high country who stole into camp that night. But we find that theory's out; the ranger staff has finished its check of everybody in that area."

"Interesting problem, then, that you've got." The manager rubbed his hands together, then passed them over his smooth dark face. "Rather hard on the members of the party, I'd say, knowing that one among them is a murderer, when there's no way to lock a tent."

A firm knock sounded on the manager's door, and at the same moment it was pushed slightly inward.

"Come in, Bertha," Alderson called out.

A middle-aged, neat woman came inside, her alert eyes taking in the occupants of the room at a glance. "You know Mr. Plummer, of course. And this is Mr. Rogers."

The woman acknowledged the introductions stiffly, and sat down on the edge of a chair which Alderson pulled out for her. "Mr. Rogers wants to ask you some questions."

"About a Mr. Wilsie who was here at the hotel for several weeks last winter," Rogers added.

"Oh, him."

"You remember him?"

"I certainly do. He had a room just two doors down the hall from old Mr. Fulton. Why, has Mr. Wilsie come back?"

"No, not that. But what can you tell me about him?"

"What do you want to know?"

"First—" and Rogers drew the photographs from his pocket—"here are two or three pictures. Is he the fellow you remember?"

The woman took the pictures apprehensively; for the first time she sensed the import of the inquiry. "I hope he's done nothing very wrong," she said. "He seemed like such a nice boy."

"But is he the fellow?" interrupted Alderson.

Bertha glanced at the pictures. She screwed up her mouth and partly closed her eyes and cocked her head. "Yes, he's the one."

"Are you sure of it?" Alderson's tone was businesslike.

"Of course. I hesitated because the pictures aren't any

too good. I mean they look like enlargements—"

"That's what they are, enlargements of a small snap-shot."

"Well, he's the fellow who was here."

"Did he say anything to you at any time about what his business was, where he came from, what his family or social connections were?"

"Oh, no, sir. He slept late usually. He and old Mr. Fulton got to be friends. He visited the old gentleman frequently after he'd been here at the hotel only a day or two."

"That's interesting," said Plummer.

"They sort of took to each other," the woman amplified.

"Did Wilsie ever say anything to you about pigeons?"

"Pigeons?" The plain face was blank. "No, I never heard him say anything about pigeons." She hesitated. "I don't know what he and Mr. Fulton talked about. Whenever I had to go into the old gentleman's room in my work while the two of them were there together they usually stopped talking and waited for me to get out."

"Did you ever notice any letters or telegrams in Wilsie's room?"

"No. He didn't throw anything in the waste basket, either."

"Did he seem nervous or uneasy?"

"He was a very calm man, I thought."

"Did he have much in the way of personal effects, clothing, I mean, or other things? I understand he carried everything away when he left. He didn't destroy anything that last day?"

"No, he didn't. Not that I know of. His clothes were

kind of skimpy for a guest at a place like this. He had some paints like an artist would have. The only other thing he had which I saw was a little green monkey about so high." She measured with her strong hands. "He said it was jade, but I don't know whether it was. He said it came from China."

The woman looked at her audience who waited for her to continue. She had answered promptly as if speaking of a guest present at the moment in the hotel instead of one gone for several months.

"Funny about this green monkey," she went on. "He had it setting out in his room all the time until just two or three days before he left. Then the green monkey showed up over in old Mr. Fulton's room. It set on his chiffonier. I never said anything to him about it, of course, but I always figured that Mr. Wilsie gave it to the old gentleman as a present."

Rogers' eyes narrowed slightly as they searched the face before him. "Is it still there?"

"I suppose so. Although I haven't been to the old gentleman's room since he left for the hike. He gave me strict orders not to come in while he was away. It was to save me work. He's like that. I made up his room, of course, that morning after he'd gone, and I didn't notice really whether the monkey was there or not."

Rogers turned to the manager. "I'd like to go up and see for myself, if I may."

"Of course. Get your keys, Bertha, and we'll go up."

"There was something else," said the maid. "I reported it at the time, Mr. Alderson. The room looked as though it had been ransacked that morning the old gentleman left on the hike. You know, little things out of place. Drawers not closed tight, and the things inside mussed up. And some of his papers on his desk scattered around. He was always such a neat man."

"That's interesting," said Plummer, running his hand through his sandy hair. Rogers made no comment.

The quartet went silently up in the elevator and along the hall to the room at the end. The maid inserted the key in the lock and threw open the door. She switched on the light and stood aside for the others to enter, and then followed them to the chiffonier against the farther wall.

"I don't see any green monkey," announced Alderson after a brief inspection.

"It ought to be right here," the maid replied, pointing to a spot beside a small alarm clock. "He's kept it right here ever since Mr. Wilsie went away, just as if he treasured it as a keepsake."

"Could it be in a drawer?" asked Alderson.

"I'll see, sir—if it's all right."

"I think it's important," said Rogers.

"Take a look, then, Bertha. Don't disturb his things."

The woman searched through all the drawers of the chiffonier, and after a few moments turned to Rogers with a gesture of upturned palms. "You see, sir, it's gone."

"Try the desk."

The maid went to the desk and looked through the drawers deftly. On Rogers' insistence the search was extended to other parts of the room where it might have been put.

"As I say, sir, it's gone," repeated the maid.

13

THE maid snapped off the light and locked the door. Rogers thanked her and she smiled and disappeared. Alderson obviously was curious and so was the chief ranger, but neither pressed him for an explanation.

"If I can be of any further service to you, Professor," the manager said as they went down to the lobby together, "please tell me."

"Thank you."

Alderson started to turn away, then glanced out of doors to where a uniformed ranger was just finishing an illustrated talk on the wild life of Yosemite to the guests assembled on the terrace.

"It's time for the fire fall, Professor. Don't you want to go out and see it?"

"Come on, Hunt; this is old stuff to us. Maybe you'd enjoy it, though."

"I always enjoy seeing it."

They stepped outside in the darkness. The high rim of the Valley was like a black shoulder blotting out the stars. Hotel guests were sitting in the darkness staring expectantly at a tiny light on Glacier Point more than 3,000 feet above the Valley floor. Faintly there came the sound of the voice at the fire on Glacier answering the call from Camp Curry below, which latter was blotted out at the hotel by the intervening trees.

"For sixty years they've been doing it. Hollering back and forth, then shoving the embers over. It's a tradition," said Plummer.

His voice had scarcely ceased when the pinpoint of light lengthened downward silently in the darkness until it became a fiery streamer, as burning embers from the bonfire kindled nightly at Glacier Point were pushed over the edge to fall a thousand feet onto a rocky ledge below. It broadened, grew brighter, glowing like the tail of a comet, then gradually dimmed and faded in silence.

The lights came on and the crowd on the terrace stirred. Rogers turned inside to the lobby, Plummer following.

"I think I ought to be getting back to Tuolumne Meadows, Floyd."

"Not tonight!"

"Yes."

"But I don't see how you can. It's seventy miles, and it's after nine o'clock."

"I'm sorry, but—"

"Now, listen, Hunt. This thing will keep till morning, surely."

"I hope it will."

"You haven't any hunches, have you, that things are not right?"

"I wouldn't call it a hunch, but I ought to get back as soon as possible."

"Now, listen. You spend the night down here with me, and I'll go up with you in the morning. I've decided I'll go the rest of the way with the hiking party. It will do me good to take the last three days of the hike."

Claudia Benson started away in high spirits from camp at Tuolumne Meadows. The sun was bright and the air invigorating. She had had the most restful night since the hike started from Happy Isles. It was because she had gone into the dormitory tent with the other single women, and had felt safer. No more sleeping in a tent alone for her after what had happened at Vogelsang.

Ahead of her along the trail the hikers were already beginning to stretch out. Professor Rogers had departed rather mysteriously the afternoon before with the chief ranger and had not returned. Nobody seemed to know whether he would rejoin the party or not. The hikers had had a pleasant evening about the campfire. Mr. Turley had tuned up a guitar belonging to a ranger and had sung ballads to them, ballads that he had collected from no one knew where. She wondered how he managed to play so well with the tip of his index finger gone.

"I'm going to be lonely today," said a voice. She turned about and then her heart sank as she saw Doug Kramer coming rapidly up.

"Am I supposed to go all soft or something with sympathy?" she said. It sounded worse than she had intended, but it didn't have any effect upon him.

"The beauteous radio singer is no longer with us."

"I heard last night that the blisters finally had got her down."

"She hopes to thumb a ride to the Valley floor."

"Good luck to her."

"And something else. It just happened."

"What?"

"The DeWitts are going to thumb too. He can't stand it. The charley horses have got him."

"I'm sorry to hear it."

"It's her nagging. She's done nothing but hack at his morale ever since we got started. But you know why,

don't you?" He went on when she made no response:
"There was a new fur coat in it if he couldn't walk all
the way around. I overheard him tell Jack Hammond that
it would be cheap at half the price to get her to let up.
He'd buy her two fur coats if he could only climb under
the wheel again. Charley horses are his way out, sort of
a defense mechanism."

Curiously, Claudia thought, Doug Kramer had been
more like himself the last day; he wasn't the impossible
creature that he had been down in San Francisco. She
wondered why he had irritated her so. Maybe, though, it
had been her fault, for she had been working hard. She
fingered the jade monkey in the pocket of her breeches;
it felt smooth and soft, almost silky to the touch. She
was going to make an opportunity on the hike today to
give it back to Mr. Fulton. Once the evening before about
the campfire she had thought of doing so, but there had
been no chance. She had puzzled all the previous afternoon
about the queer way he had taken to wish the thing upon
her.

"Do you get this Forbes dame?" asked Doug of a
sudden.

"How do you mean, Doug?"

"She's too smooth. I can't make her out. Most of the
others—Beryl Lindsay, say, and Mrs. DeWitt—are like
open books, but the more you try to penetrate Miss Forbes
the deeper she gets and the farther she recedes into the
background."

"Do you know anything about her?"

He didn't answer her directly. He said: "She's started
sniping at old man Fulton. Talking to him, I mean. There's
something going on. You watch her. She reminds me of

a cat getting all set to spring on an unsuspecting bird. Which I imagine the old man is, in this instance, an unsuspecting old bird."

"Do you know anything about Mr. Fulton?" Claudia realized she was gossiping, and tried to pull herself out of it.

"Yes, he's the old man who has rowed in court with all his wives and children and nieces and nephews. Finally paid them all off and retired to the Ahwahnee."

"Oh, I remember something in our files about him; I didn't realize he was the one. But I'm not supposed to tell any clients' secrets."

"I'm not asking you to. You don't know anything about him that I don't know. I probably could tell you things."

"You don't have to be so short about it."

"All right, go ahead and flare up. Who asked about old man Fulton in the first place?"

Claudia walked away from Douglas Kramer. That was the way it usually ended. Their tempers were too much alike. She'd be better off to let him alone for the rest of the day.

"Good morning, Mr. Milbank," said Claudia catching up with the park naturalist. "I haven't spoken to you yet this morning."

"Good morning, Miss Benson. Sleep all right?"

"Fine."

"Really enjoying the hike, aren't you?"

"Tremendously. I'm not going to want to quit when the time is up."

"That's normal. Most hikers when they get to the end would like to start right out and walk around the loop again."

"Where's Professor Rogers? I missed him last night."

"He couldn't make it back to camp. He's coming today, though. I had word from them late last night. Mr. Plummer is coming along too for the rest of the trip. If they don't overtake us on the trail, they'll follow on into Glen Aulin this afternoon."

"Is it about the death of Mr. Hodges—they're still trying to solve it?"

"Naturally they won't quit until something's found out. You don't happen to have learned anything of importance?"

"Not a thing. Nobody has done anything suspicious in my presence. The DeWitts—"

"What about them?"

"They're not going any farther, I hear."

Bruce Milbank gave her an odd look. "He says he's fed up with walking," he remarked with a tone of finality, then changed the subject. "This is a short hike today. I'm going to suggest to those who feel equal to it to follow the Tuolumne on down below Glen Aulin this afternoon. We don't go that way tomorrow."

"What's there to see?"

"The upside down falls. Ridges and depressions in the river bed throw the waters in arcs thirty to forty feet," he explained, "and they look like waterfalls in reverse."

"I'll go."

"It will add several miles. I wish we could go as far as Waterwheel. But that's too much."

"Extra miles don't scare me now that I'm broken in to it."

Old Mr. Fulton seemed purposely avoiding Claudia.

He appeared to have joined with Frederick Dudley and Jack Hammond for the day. She walked hopefully near them for a couple of miles, expecting the trio to split up, but it did not. She stopped and took part in the conversation when they sat down for a ten-minute rest, but finally she gave it up.

Beryl Lindsay was teaching Mr. Turley an Ozark Mountain ballad when she came up to them on the trail. Miss Lindsay's voice was not musical, but she made up for it in enthusiasm. The two were sitting together against the trunk of a lodgepole pine when Claudia discovered them. They invited her to sit down and all three sat singing the song until the others were far ahead of them. Although they hurried to overtake the party when Turley was satisfied that he had learned the ballad, they did not catch up with the other hikers until they reached Glen Aulin.

It was not until mid-afternoon that Claudia found Thomas Fulton alone. The party had rested at camp and then started to see the falls below Glen Aulin. The old man was sitting on a rock in a grove of aspens whose trunks were scarred with clawmarks where bears were accustomed to take their morning stretch. The elderly man looked lonely and forsaken.

"I don't think I'll go on with the others," he said when Claudia sat down beside him.

"Oh, I'm sorry that you're not feeling up to it."

"It isn't that. I could walk from now until dark, and it wouldn't tire me."

The river flowed quietly past them through what had once been a lake bed gouged by glacial action, but long since filled in and overgrown with vegetation. A question was on the tip of Claudia's tongue when the old man spoke again.

"You're bothered about that little monkey I gave you yesterday."

"I've worried about having it. I don't understand it at all. I've already had to deceive Professor Rogers."

"How's that?"

"I talked with him after you gave the monkey back to me. He'd heard about what happened at Vogelsang. But I told him it was just some more of my horrible dreams. I couldn't tell him what it was all about, after you'd asked me to say nothing. It's a bit embarrassing. I think I ought to give it back to you."

"Please, do me the favor of keeping it a little longer."

"I found it in my pack at Merced Lake that first afternoon."

"I put it there. I shouldn't have done it like that. But an old man isn't quick to think sometimes."

"But, why?"

"I know what happened at Vogelsang. Miss Forbes said you thought you'd been robbed, and then guessed you'd dreamed it. I know differently. But I wasn't the fellow in your tent."

"But——" Claudia was bewildered. "How did you get it back?"

"Excuse me if I sound abrupt. But I've had about all I can stand. I shouldn't have come on this hike."

"Why?" Claudia was puzzled by his sudden change of manner.

"I'd have been much better off back at the hotel. They

couldn't have got at me there the way they have on this trip."

Claudia didn't understand what the old man was talking about so she said nothing, hoping that he would explain.

"I've been hounded all my life. Now they're after me again for money. Always money. None of them ever thought of earning a dime for themselves; they look to me for it. Now they threaten me."

"I'm sorry."

"No, you're not sorry. You don't know what I'm talking about. All you're concerned about is the monkey."

Claudia pulled the little piece of jade from her pocket and gave it back to the old man. She started to get to her feet.

"Please," he said, seizing her hand and pulling her down again. "It's just a keepsake a friend gave me. He said he'd come back for it some day. Or somebody would come with a note for it. It was just a hunch that made me bring it along. It was just a hunch last Monday that made me slip it into your pack. But, now, somebody was so eager to get hold of it that he stole it from you. That's puzzled me a lot. I begin to see something in it I don't like. A lot of strange things have happened. There was a telephone call, and there was a note under my door, which I tore up. I should have kept it—"

"About the jade monkey?"

"No. About the man who gave it to me last winter. I was awake when the fellow left the dormitory tent. I've been sleeping in the dormitory tent since Hodges died. I wasn't born yesterday. I heard the fellow come back. I don't like to accuse him, for after all it may be trivial.

I didn't know what had happened, though, at the time. He dropped the monkey accidentally, as he was getting back into bed, and he hunted for it for a while. Somebody else woke up and the fellow was afraid to do any more searching. I was awake but I kept still. It landed in one of my shoes. That's how I got it again."

"Who was it?"

"The time may not come to tell the man's name. I say it's trivial, although robbing a young woman in the dead of night is serious enough. So, please, keep it for me. Something tells me it will be safe with you. I want to sound out this fellow before anything is done. And, now, you'll be left out of the party that's gone down the canyon. I'm waiting to see somebody."

"Thank you for the explanation. I'll keep it for you." Claudia thrust the piece of jade into her pocket and got to her feet. "I'll see you at dinner tonight." She smiled and turned away down stream through the aspens.

"Good-bye," the old man's voice reached her. There was something so sort of final, Claudia thought, in the way he spoke. The dispirited tone of the old voice sent a shiver down her back. It was almost as if it were forever, that she'd never see him again.

14

CHIEF RANGER PLUMMER and Huntoon Rogers walked into camp at Glen Aulin, situated at the foot of the White Cascade on the Tuolumne River. To the chief ranger it was the most restful of all the High Sierra campsites, and he liked to visit it.

"Nobody around apparently," he said to Rogers. "Oh, Ben! Ben!" he shouted for the camp host.

"Hi!" answered a voice from among the tents. A leathery-faced, stocky man soon came walking up.

"Where is everybody, Ben?"

"Hello, Mr. Plummer." The man approached and shook hands. "Why, they all went down the Tuolumne. Some of 'em figured they might go as far as Waterwheel Falls. But I doubt it. There's a couple of 'em here that didn't go. Man and his wife. DeWitt is the name. Just got in about fifteen minutes ago. I been showing 'em their tent."

"DeWitt? I understood they quit at Tuolumne Meadows."

"Well, he explained that they changed their minds. Some girl who'd dropped out caught a ride down below, they said, and then they, meaning the DeWitts, decided to come on and go the rest of the way. He says he's going to bed, though. Says his legs bother."

"Well, Hunt," Plummer turned to Rogers, "we might as well make ourselves comfortable. Unless you're hell-bent for following on the heels of the rest of them."

"I'm not. It's too comfortable here in the shade. It's a beautiful stand of mountain hemlock in here," he said to the camp host.

"Finest in the Sierras," said Ben Mayfield. "I'll show you a tent, Mr. Rogers, if you want."

"No hurry. I'll put up in the dormitory."

"That's it right down there." Mayfield pointed. "Help yourself to a bed. Some of the fellows have already claimed theirs."

"How about the old gentleman, Ben? Old Mr. Fulton?"

"Oh, he went with the rest of the crowd."

"Remarkable!" exclaimed Plummer. "He's going to see it all."

The chief ranger was disappointed. He had hoped to arrive at Glen Aulin before the party scattered for the afternoon. On the way up he had discussed with Rogers the advisability of further interrogation at once of Leon Mullins. There were things that didn't square in the man's statements at Merced Lake, which Rogers had pointed out to him. But, now, there was nothing to be done until the party returned. He was feeling sleepy and so he sat down in a shady spot and dozed. Rogers was stretched out with his hat over his face.

It was not until he smelled the odors from the kitchen range and heard the rattle of dishes heralding the approach of the dinner hour that he roused completely. The first few hikers were beginning to straggle in from the lower trail. Rogers had disappeared. There was a stir about the camp as more hikers came in and they prepared for dinner. They looked tired, but their spirits were excellent. The party had shaken down as he was sure it would, even despite the terrific jolt it had sustained at Merced

Lake. He saw Bruce Milbank coming in with Miss Lindsay and Douglas Kramer, and he went over to the naturalist.

"Hello," Milbank said. "Looked for you earlier, Mr. Plummer."

"We couldn't make it. Mr. Haverly had something on his mind that delayed us."

"Did Professor Rogers come up with you?"

"Yes. Where's Mr. Fulton?"

"He's already back, I guess. We're the last of the party."

"I haven't seen him."

"I'll take a look." Milbank disappeared among the tents and came back within a few minutes.

"I don't find him," he said. "His pack is in the dormitory. But he left it there, of course, before he started down the river with us. He'll show up. I didn't think, though, that we could miss him on the trail."

Plummer sat down at the table. Miss Forbes, he noted, managed to sit between Rogers and himself, as she had at Merced Lake. He didn't object, of course, for she was an entertaining talker.

"I'm just a bit worried about Mr. Fulton," he said to her, as he noted the still vacant seat at the table.

"I wonder— I talked with him this afternoon."

"Where?"

"A couple of miles below here. Down in that forest of aspens. It's lovely down in there, isn't it?"

Plummer thought the matter of Fulton's absence worthy of greater attention, so he lifted his voice to the hikers at table.

"Does anybody know what's become of Mr. Fulton?"

Nobody did. There were blank looks and shaking heads.

"Did he go with you to the falls?"

"Not all the way," Milbank answered. "Only four of us went below California Fall. Miss Lindsay, Mr. Kramer, Mr. Dudley, and I made it almost to Le Conte. Of the others, I think they most of them got as far as California Fall. We picked them up on the way back. Did Mr. Fulton get as far as California Fall?" Milbank asked generally.

"I think he did," replied Ralph Stoner. "I was fishing in a pool below there. Good fishing too—" and he indicated his plate and those of several others filled with fried trout. "The book says you can't find anything much in there, but I found 'em."

"What about Mr. Fulton, though?" Milbank urged,

"I saw him above the falls. He hung around there a little while, then disappeared. That's all I know."

"Was anybody with him?"

"Oh, there were others up there too. Jack Hammond, Miss Forbes, Mullins. I didn't keep track of who all came and went."

The chief ranger thought the inquiry was too pro-tracted, for at any moment he expected the old man to walk in to dinner. Rogers ate quietly, seeming to pay little attention to the conversation.

"I didn't mean to be too inquisitive with you folks about Mr. Fulton," Plummer said, dismissing the matter. "I was just wondering what was keeping him."

"I for one," began Miss Forbes, addressing Plummer, "don't think a man as old as Mr. Fulton should undertake such strenuous things as he's doing. He's too old."

"That's what the superintendent thinks," Plummer answered. "He didn't think so at first. Now he wants to send up a saddle horse, just in case Mr. Fulton should get overtired on the last half of this trip. It was all I could do to talk him out of it. The old fellow would never forgive him if he did. From what I hear of his performance so far, I think Mr. Fulton's marvelous. He'll walk all the way home; that's my prediction."

"I hope you're right. Leon Mullins offered to bet that he would make it, but I didn't take him up."

"You'd have lost your money if you had," Plummer laughed.

"Yes, and I can't afford to lose any money betting."

The dinner plates were removed, and the dessert put upon the table, and still Thomas Fulton had not come to dinner. With each succeeding mouthful of his dessert the conviction grew in the chief ranger's mind that the old man wasn't coming to dinner. The sun was below the mountain peaks, the dark shadow of Falls Ridge enfolded the camp in semi-darkness. Plummer got up from the table, leaving part of his dessert untouched and his second cup of coffee untasted.

The eyes of the hikers watched him disappear through the doorway. Rogers got up and followed the chief ranger outside. They went down to the dormitory tent and found it empty. They beat about the grounds outside the tents. Plummer called the old man's name once, but there was no response. All the while Rogers said nothing. They turned back toward the dining tent.

"We'll need flashlights, Hunt," remarked Plummer.

"I've got mine in my pocket."

"Ben probably has several. Bruce has one, I know. Bruce oughtn't to go, though, if he's been almost to Le Conte Fall. That's enough hiking for one day—and the fellows who were with him too. The others, some of them, probably can stand a little more. Sorry now that I argued with Mr. Haverly about the old man. He's given out somewhere along the trail. Maybe had a heart attack. It's pretty strenuous work hiking over mountain trails."

"Why don't you say what you think, Floyd?"

"I'm afraid to, Hunt. I'm hoping that what I've been saying is the truth."

Milbank joined them, and Turley and Hammond came up.

"Shouldn't we start looking for Mr. Fulton?" Milbank asked.

"I'm starting just as soon as we can get flashlights, and a few men to help. But, Bruce, you've had a pretty hard day. Better stay here."

"I'm good for another ten miles."

The crowd was pouring outside into the dusk. The chief ranger lifted his voice slightly.

"If any of you people have flashlights and want to come along, we're going to take a little hike down the trail to see if we can meet Mr. Fulton. He's miscalculated the time it would take to get back to camp."

Nobody really believed that that was true, but Plummer was pleased that they accepted it without question. A few minutes later, with flashlights picking out the trail, the party set off.

"I should think, Mr. Plummer," said Milbank at the chief ranger's elbow, "that if we go as far as California Fall, that will be far enough. If he isn't on the trail, then on the way back we'd better fan out through the glen just in case he's wandered from the trail into the aspens."

"Sounds logical, Bruce."

For a while there was only the sound of heavy shoes

upon the hard trail and the murmur of voices from the
rear rank of the searchers, some of whom already were
walking wide of the trail. In the area where the river became quiet as it meandered through the aspens, the chief
ranger halted the searchers in a group and requested silence. He then raised his voice in a long drawn-out call to
the old man. His voice echoed waveringly through the
gloom and was thrown back from the steep sides of the
mountain walls. Nobody spoke as they strained their ears
to detect an answering voice. The call was repeated several
times, but there was no answer.

They went on, flashing their lights upon the trail and
among the trees to either side. An air of tense, grim purpose seemed to have settled upon the searchers. They had
been inclined at one point to joke among themselves; at
last they had got something on the old man about which
they could tease him. But that stopped after a short while.

Suddenly there was a startled snuffling among the shadows, a grunt, then a heavy body went crashing away in the
darkness. The searchers halted in alarm, then somebody
laughed, and that eased the tension that had tightened in
their throats.

"Just a bear," said Milbank jokingly. "He's probably
more scared than you are."

They went on, and nervous laughter ran like a ripple
among the searchers. The party became even more dili-
gent in its search; the darkness deepened until it seemed
as though a black curtain had dropped its smothering folds
about them. The distant roar of waterfalls was subdued
and like a breath of wind in the pines.

"How far have we gone?" asked Hammond from the
rear. His voice sounded tremulous.

"Couple of miles, probably," Milbank answered.

"He wouldn't be this far, I don't think."

"How do you know, Jack?" Stoner retorted.

"I just thought he wouldn't; he's an old man."

"If he got dazed, say, maybe he'd wander away from camp instead of toward it," suggested Frederick Dudley.

The chief ranger called out. "We're going as far as California Fall, men. Then we'll spread out on the way back."

"What's keeping us? Let's go," urged Hammond.

A voice came from the rear and slightly off the trail. There was a note of sudden alarm in it. A flashlight was waved as if in a signal.

"Who's that off there?" asked Plummer.

"Sounds like DeWitt's voice," answered Milbank. "What is it?" he shouted.

"I've found him."

The searchers instantly abandoned the trail and went crashing through the undergrowth. Nobody spoke as they sought to gain the spot now marked by a steady vertical beam of the flashlight. Branches of the trees jabbed at them, clutched, held them back; they stumbled over the rough ground.

"Here! This way!" directed DeWitt. "There's a little trail. Deer trail, I guess. You can come right here on it."

"Is it Mr. Fulton?" asked Milbank anxiously.

"That's how I happened to find him. I followed this little trail to see where it went, and here he was on the ground."

"Is he all right?" demanded Plummer.

For a moment there was no answer. Flashlights were trained on the thin form at their feet which seemed to huddle on the ground as if in fear.

"I don't think so," answered DeWitt. "He doesn't say anything when I speak to him. He just lays there."

"Mr. Fulton!" Plummer's voice was anxious. "Mr. Fulton, are you all right?" The chief ranger dropped beside the figure. He touched the cheek, the chest, then felt for the pulse. Slowly he got to his feet. "No," he said, "he's not all right. He's dead."

15

CLAUDIA BENSON took her seat with the others in the chairs placed about the campfire just outside the dining tent. She shivered a little. The flames which had been leaping brightly were dying down, leaving the embers glowing like hot gold. And still nothing was said about what had happened. She had seen the men come back from the search, and had been shocked by the news about old Mr. Fulton. She had suddenly felt lonely and afraid, and she couldn't help thinking of the old man as he sat among the aspens earlier that afternoon and called good-bye to her as if he never expected to see her again.

They had brought the body back, and she had turned her face away when it was carried to a tent apart from the others. Then Chief Ranger Plummer telephoned the news to the Valley floor. She'd heard him direct that a pack horse be brought over the next morning from Tuolumne Meadows. There had been a touch of hard authority in these developments; the free, easy feeling of comradeship about the campfire had vanished. There was now something grim in the air. And there was over all a sense of loneliness she had never experienced before. The dark hemlocks, the great mass of mountains seemed to shut them completely off from human things. Although the Tioga Road was only five or six miles away, night had closed down, and there probably was no travel on it, and the Valley floor, where everything was gay and there were crowds, was miles and miles away. Seventy, somebody had said, by the highway, and it had been a four-days' hike the way they had come. They seemed locked in an unfriendly wilderness.

Suddenly the chief ranger and Professor Rogers sat down in the circle about the fire. Those who had been talking ceased as if they had been ordered to stop. All eyes were upon the pair. They were tired from their exertions, as was nearly everybody else; only Mrs. DeWitt seemed fresh.

"I'll waste no time in preliminaries," said the chief ranger. His voice sounded harsh. "You all know what's happened, and must have some idea of what it means. It's necessary to say, as some of you are aware already, that Mr. Fulton didn't die of a stroke, or heart attack—or anything as pleasant as that. It's much worse, a much grimmer, dirtier business. A skull fracture, to be frank with you, was the cause of death, inflicted by someone who sought and succeeded in accomplishing the old man's death. Since he had to die, I had been hoping before we found him that it would be from a heart attack, or at worst a fall. But, no, nothing like that. Just as Harry Hodges met his death at Merced Lake, so has Mr. Fulton come to his end."

He paused for his words to sink in. Claudia bit her lips, and a cold hand seemed to be laid upon her back. She stared into the fire where the glowing embers were sending out waves of warmth, the only thing of cheerful aspect in the darkness and the hard circumstance that had fallen upon them.

"I regret what has happened even more than you do," Plummer went on. "I regret that this unfortunate happening has further interfered with your pleasure. But you will understand the necessity the park service is under in arriving at the fullest possible explanation of Mr. Fulton's death. Whoever among you is responsible, I mean to find out who you are. Or, if it is not one of you, then whoever that person is who may have followed you into the back country to pick off his victims, I mean to find him. My friend here—Professor Rogers—is as interested as I am in the matter. I am asking him, as at Merced Lake, to help me with the investigation I propose to undertake while everything is fresh in all our minds.

"Now, then, who last saw Mr. Fulton, and where?"

Impelled by some inexplicable force, Claudia Benson spoke up. "I saw him on the trail, Mr. Plummer, this afternoon. It was among the aspens. I sat down and talked with him, then I went on and caught up with the others, at the California Fall. I didn't see him when I came back."

"What time was it when you talked with him?"

"I'd guess it was about four o'clock. I didn't look at my watch. But he was sitting there as our part of the crowd came along, and I dropped out to talk to him."

"Was there anything significant in your conversation, Claudia?" Rogers asked quietly.

"Well—" she hesitated. "After a while he said he was expecting someone to come and talk with him. So I left. And he said good-bye in such a way that it sounded like forever."

An odd silence ensued. Claudia shivered slightly with the recollection. Beryl Lindsay who sat at her elbow threw an extra sweater over Claudia's shoulders, and she was grateful for the added warmth.

"Did he indicate whom he expected to talk to?"

"Only that it might be a relative."

"A relative?"

"He got to talking about how his relatives had hounded him for money all their lives. It was dreadfully on his mind. Maybe I misunderstood."

Professor Rogers addressed the group in general. "Is it worth-while asking the question: Is there a relative of Mr. Fulton among you people?" He looked inquiringly about.

Miss Forbes who sat across the fire from Claudia threw her half-smoked cigarette into the fire. She cleared her throat softly.

"I don't see any reason for holding it back now," she began. There was a faint suggestion of nervousness in her voice. "It will be in all the papers anyway as soon as the news of his death gets out that I—well, not to beat about the bush, I am a niece of Thomas Fulton, his only sister's child. And we haven't spoken for ten years, until this afternoon when I had a talk with him on the trail below here, just as Miss Benson has indicated."

There was an acid inflection in her voice when she pronounced Claudia's name, and all Claudia's feeling of friendliness toward Miss Forbes suddenly vanished. It was as if she had accused Claudia of meddling in her affairs.

"Will you tell us—" began Rogers.

"I'll tell you nothing of the conversation I had with Uncle Tom," Miss Forbes flashed rudely. "That's beside the point, strictly personal, and can't possibly have had anything to do with his death. Our talk didn't last ten minutes. After it was over, I turned around and came back to camp alone. I left him sitting on that rock. If you doubt me, ask Mrs. Mayfield if I didn't come back fully an hour before the rest of you began to straggle in."

There was an air of defiance in her words. The light

from the campfire shone upon her well-shaped head. Her nostrils widened a trifle, and there was a glitter in her dark eyes.

"One more question, Miss Forbes," Rogers persisted. "Do you stand to profit by your uncle's death?"

"Profit?" the word was sharp. It had been forced from her against her will. For a moment it was plain that she was undecided whether to say more, then suddenly she added: "I hope so. There was a time when I was his principal heir. I came before his own children. But I fell from grace. I'll probably get a dollar." Her lips clamped firmly on the final word.

"Thank you," said Rogers quietly.

"May I offer an alibi in this thing, Mr. Rogers?" a voice broke in upon the sudden silence.

"Alibis are always in order." Rogers turned to Kramer.

"I was with Bruce Milbank from the time we left camp right after lunch until we got back just before dinner time."

"He's right about that, Professor," Milbank affirmed soberly. "Miss Lindsay, Mr. Kramer, and Mr. Dudley went with me almost to Le Conte Fall."

"All the way back with you?" the chief ranger asked.

"Yes, sir. Excepting Mr. Dudley. He fell by the wayside a couple of miles or so below here."

"The pace was a little too fast for me," Dudley explained with an uneasy smile. "I dropped out for a ten-minute rest, then came on in a little slower. How do you do it, Miss Lindsay?" he inquired casually of the school teacher.

"I've been a great walker all my life. I love it."

"Let's go back, though, to Mr. Fulton," persisted Rogers.

"Yes?" Dudley was deliberate. "If you mean did I see the old gentleman? Do I know anything about his unfortunate end? Do I have any suspicions as to who may be guilty? No to all of them. I haven't the slightest idea how to help you. I'm sorry."

"Thank you," Rogers responded. "And Mr. Turley, what can you tell us?"

"Very little." The man was smoking his pipe. He removed the pipe stem from his lips. "I'm one of those unfortunate individuals who never seem to be at the exact center of excitement when anything happens. I always have to get it second hand."

"But did you see anything of Mr. Fulton? Talk with him? See anything suspicious while you were on the trail this afternoon?"

"No, sir. I didn't get as far as the first fall, which most of the others seem to have done. I thought to myself, what's the use? I loafed along the river, smoked and communed with Nature."

"Now, I'll tell you about myself," broke in Jack Hammond.

Claudia thought he was too eager to be heard. She had not got over her first reaction to him at Merced Lake. She didn't like him as an individual; she didn't like his type. He had never stopped sniping at her, though.

"What about yourself?" Plummer asked.

"I'm in the clear. I went to the first fall. I saw Stoner fishing. I said good-bye to the guys letting themselves in for the hike down to the falls below, then I turned around and came back."

"Did you see Mr. Fulton at the first fall?"

"No, sir."

"At dinner Mr. Stoner said he saw the old gentleman there."

"Well, now, maybe I was mistaken," Stoner broke in emphatically. "I know I said it, but I got to thinking about it later, and I'm not so sure. I could have been mistaken."

"You said several persons came and went as you fished."

"I ain't denying it. Maybe the fellow that I thought was Fulton was somebody else. I had my mind on fishing."

"Mr. Hammond," the chief ranger inquired, "on your way back did you see anybody who now could confirm your statement that you came directly to camp?"

"DeWitt was wandering around down there among the trees."

"You're mistaken, my friend," DeWitt challenged coldly. "I'm not doing any extra hiking on this trip. My wife and I nearly quit you at Tuolumne Meadows. Oh, no, you couldn't have seen me."

"I sure thought I did."

"Ask my wife. She'll tell you I didn't get far from camp."

"Why put it up to me?" Mrs. DeWitt inquired tartly of her husband. "I slept all afternoon. I don't know where you wandered to."

"Well, I didn't go down there where the old man died."

"You seemed to know how to find him when the rest of us couldn't." The retort came from Stoner in one corner of whose mouth lurked a sly grin that Claudia did not like.

"What if I did find him? That only goes to show that my eyes are sharper than yours, and that I use my head instead of my feet."

Claudia thought she saw Professor Rogers nudge the chief ranger and settle back in his chair as if to let the argument run its course. There was a quickening of interest about the circle as the two thrust at each other.

"You don't happen to be a relative of the old gentleman, too, do you, DeWitt?" retorted Stoner.

"Never saw him in all my life before last Monday. Of course, I'd read about him. Who hasn't?"

"We're not getting anywhere arguing like this. If it wasn't you I saw over there in the trees when I came back to camp, then who was it? It wasn't Leon here." Hammond laid a hand upon the cowboy's arm. "I left him sitting on a rock back along the trail, didn't I, Leon?"

"Yes," answered Mullins. "You asked me if I was going to camp then. I said I wasn't ready yet."

"Waiting to talk to the old gentleman, were you?" asked DeWitt. To Claudia it seemed like a chance remark, but it could have been calculated to direct attention away from himself.

"I'd already talked with Mr. Fulton," replied Mullins quietly. He held one knee in his clasped hands and stared at the fire.

"Tell us about it," urged Plummer.

"There isn't much to tell, Mr. Plummer. We talked personal things mostly. Sort of odds and ends like two fellows would talk after being on the trail together for four days."

"Did he express any fears for his life? You remember what Miss Benson said a while ago that he said good-bye to her as if he didn't expect to see her again."

"He didn't express any fears to me, Mr. Plummer. He seemed natural."

"How did you leave him?"

"He left me. Just got up and said he'd see me again. I've noticed Mr. Fulton didn't waste words."

"Did you see Mr. Dudley returning to camp?"

"He went by a little while after Mr. Fulton left me. Asked me to go along, but I said I wasn't ready yet."

"Is that true, Mr. Dudley?" the chief ranger inquired.

"Yes."

"Did you overtake Mr. Fulton on the trail to camp?"

"I didn't see him anywhere."

"Were you ahead or behind Mr. Stoner?"

Stoner answered. "I was cleaning fish when he came in."

"Did you see anything of Mr. DeWitt along the trail?"

"No, sir. I saw Mr. Turley sitting on the river bank smoking. He and Mullins were the only two I saw on the last stretch."

"Well," said the chief ranger after a moment's silence, "we don't seem to have learned much, except what you were all doing at the time we are interested in."

16

THERE was a stir among the hikers about the campfire, as if the chief ranger's words had signaled the end of the inquiry. Claudia drew her feet under her, thankful that it was over and glad of the opportunity to go to bed. She was puzzled and not a little disappointed that the inquiry had been so barren of result. The fact that a murderer could strike among them with impunity filled her with a vague sort of dread; were any of them safe now after what had happened? She got to her feet and looked about, expecting someone else to follow her example, but instead Beryl Lindsay's voice broke the sudden silence that had fallen upon them.

"I don't think we ought to give up so easily. If the person who killed that fine old man is sitting here in this circle, I think we ought to know who he or she is before we break up tonight."

"I agree with you, Miss Lindsay," said William Turley promptly, as if he were seconding a routine motion at a prosaic business meeting.

"Have you any suggestions as to how we should next proceed, Miss Lindsay?" inquired the chief ranger.

"For one, I'd like to know what was ever done about the death of Mr. Hodges. So far as I know, that's never been explained. Have we been associating with a double murderer all the way from Happy Isles? Are the two crimes connected? Did the same person do both? And why was the half leaf torn out of my notebook at Merced Lake when I left it on the bench? Does it have anything to do with either crime? And why did Mr. and Mrs. DeWitt change their minds and follow along after the party when they'd said they were going to quit? Maybe I'm putting my foot in it with some of these questions, but it's time somebody got his foot into it——"

"You certainly have put your foot in it, old girl!" began May DeWitt icily. "If you infer that because Al and I changed our minds and tagged along over here to Glen Aulin, it has something to do with either killing——I'll——" She clenched her small hands impotently.

A faint smile flickered on Rogers' lips. Beryl Lindsay, instead of resenting Mrs. DeWitt's retort, smiled broadly if not a bit smugly at the thin blond woman who sat beside her husband.

"I'll tell you how it was," Al DeWitt rushed to his wife's support. "I just couldn't be a quitter. I'd signed up to go all the way around, and I'm going. I've had trouble with my legs. They ain't what they used to be, so I ought to be given some credit for my courage, don't you think? It's the old never-say-die spirit. Now, does that satisfy everybody?"

"No," said Miss Lindsay bluntly.

"Well——" DeWitt shrugged his shoulders, "I've done the best I can, lady."

"Maybe you got to thinking about that fur coat you'd be stuck for, Al," laughed Jack Hammond.

"What do you know about a fur coat?" demanded May DeWitt with a show of temper. She turned upon her husband. "Al, did you tell this awful person about that?" Her voice betrayed her anger and she seized her husband by the arm as if he were a small boy.

"Oh, keep still. What difference does it make? You were

telling the girls down in Oakland about the bet—"

"Well, the girls in Oakland are one thing and this—this Hammond person is something else."

"Oh, is that so? Don't care for my style. High hat!"

"Just a minute, please," broke in the chief ranger. "Personalities, I'm afraid, won't help us much. I've tried to make this as easy as possible. I know you're all tired. You've had a hard day, but if anybody knows anything about Mr. Fulton's death—or Mr. Hodges'—by all means let's have it."

"Mr. Plummer, we resent having anybody interpret our actions," began DeWitt calmly, "either our deciding to go the rest of the hike, or what I may have been doing this afternoon on the trail below here—"

"So you admit that you were down there!" Miss Lindsay pounced upon him. "A while ago you were denying it. You said you didn't leave camp."

DeWitt's jaw dropped. "I had my reasons," he mumbled quickly.

"What were they?" asked Plummer.

"They haven't anything to do with the old man's death."

"Did you see him?"

"Well—yes. I saw him. Talked with him."

"And you say it has nothing to do with his death?" The chief ranger was mildly incredulous.

"That's right. Although you probably think it did. And so I wanted to keep still about it. You'd get a wrong impression. If the old man hadn't been murdered—well, you might as well know. I'll tell it to you and you'll get it straight then; if you get it from somewhere else, it'll be wrong.

"It's like this," he said, looking anxiously at his wife,

who sat as if carved of stone. "I've got to tell 'em, now, May——" He turned back to Plummer. "My wife's name before I married her was Fulton. She was the old man's daughter by his first marriage. The two of them hadn't spoken for years."

"I knew it! I knew it!" exclaimed Beryl Lindsay.

"Oh, you did!" snapped DeWitt sarcastically.

"Anybody could see the resemblance. I've got a genius for that, though." The school teacher crowed with delight.

"Now, let me explain things." DeWitt was like a drowning man clutching at a straw. "We came on this hike at the old man's invitation. He wrote and asked us to come. He'd pay the expense——"

"You see," interrupted May DeWitt with a rush of information, "he'd fought us all for years in court and out, and cut us off, and been as mean as he could be to us. The invitation was out of a clear sky. Naturally we wondered what was behind it. He played on our curiosity. We didn't dare not come. But we kept looking for the joker. That's why we were late at the rendezvous at Happy Isles Monday morning. We went around by the Ahwahnee that morning to find out if he was really going. We still thought there might be a trick. But they told us he'd already left for the rendezvous." She finished with an air as if she had said the final word.

"By the way, Mr. DeWitt," Rogers asked, "had you had no conversation with Mr. Fulton up until this afternoon?"

"No more than just a howdy-do. He didn't seem to want to talk to either May or me. We thought he'd changed his mind about whatever he had to say to us, and wished we hadn't come."

"Was that why you dropped out at Tuolumne Meadows this morning?"

"Partly. Then we got scared that we'd offend him, and decided to have a showdown as to what was on his mind. So we came along here to Glen Aulin. They told me he'd gone down the trail, so I left May at the tent and started out to find him."

"What was the result?" Rogers asked.

"It was a friendly talk. Surprised me. I'd never known the old man. He'd never recognized me as a son-in-law, you understand. The talk was all about his getting old, and maybe he'd been wrong, or, at least, as wrong as his family had been. I was encouraged."

"And the fur coat business—" Jack Hammond interrupted.

"That was just a side bet," DeWitt said testily. "As I say, I was quite encouraged."

"Well, that was more than I was after I'd talked to him." The words came from Miss Forbes.

"Yeah?" DeWitt said.

"You were invited," Miss Forbes continued. "You and May. I wasn't. That's where I made my mistake. I came up to Yosemite hoping to see Uncle Tom and have a talk with him, but I didn't have any luck. He wouldn't talk to me. He instructed the hotel not to take any telephone calls from me, even; he didn't want to talk on the phone with me. Only by accident did I learn that he was coming on this hike, and I said to myself, here's where I put it over on him. I'll go along."

"Had you talked with him before today?" Rogers asked.

"No. I finally told him this morning that I was going to talk to him, and he said all right, later." She stopped all of a sudden, having hurried through with what she had to say as if speed in telling her story would bolster its credibility.

"Well—" Rogers broke the silence that followed. A smile played about his lips. "I suppose that you three people who are related to Mr. Fulton realize that you have established motives for yourselves as his slayer."

"Oh, I say," protested Miss Forbes, "that's not fair."

"I only point out the fact. Mr. Fulton was wealthy, I understand."

"Millionaire," said DeWitt quickly.

"And, I presume," put in Plummer, "that both you, Miss Forbes, and you, Mrs. DeWitt, will inherit a share of the money."

"Not I!" exclaimed Miss Forbes. "He cut me off years ago."

"Did he say so today?"

"The subject of inheritance wasn't even mentioned. I wouldn't be so tactless as to bring it up, if I was expecting to get into his good graces again, would I? If I was hoping to patch things up, I wouldn't go around waving a reg flag in front of a bull, so to speak, would I? Not if I was intelligent. And I submit that I am intelligent."

"Oh, there's no doubt of it, Miss Forbes," Plummer hastened to say.

"How about you, Al?" asked Hammond. "Did you ask the old man how much you and the missus was going to get when he kicked off?"

May DeWitt bit her lips and turned her face away, staring into the dark shadows beyond the fire. Her husband replied with elaborate patience: "As I said before, Jack, we didn't talk about anything except that things had been bad between him and his folks in the past, and that it was regrettable, now that he was old and might enjoy the company of his family. Money wasn't mentioned. Not once. He didn't even ask me how I was doing, or whether I was making a good living for May, or how I was fixed financially. You don't suppose that in the first real conversation I had ever had with him I'd be dumb enough to start harping on money? And was he going to leave May anything? You're nuts if you think I'm that crazy."

"Okay, okay, I was just asking to be polite," Hammond retorted.

"Better keep your mouth shut about things that don't concern you."

"It don't concern me that I may be the next one killed?" Hammond's voice soared to a shrill note of incredulity. "I'll say it concerns everybody in this crowd who hopes to get back alive to the Valley floor."

"We're getting a bit off the subject," Rogers said. "Another question, Mr. DeWitt."

"Yeah?"

"You say you went to the Ahwahnee before you joined the party Monday morning, to see if Mr. Fulton was really going."

"Yes; what about it?"

"Did either you or Mrs. DeWitt go up to his room?"

"Up to his room?" Al DeWitt seemed irritated by the question.

"Yes, up to Mr. Fulton's room?"

"What do you think we are, anyway? Just in from the country? No, we didn't go up to his room. We asked at the desk, when we couldn't get him on the house phone, and they said he'd already left for Happy Isles, and so we beat it up to the rendezvous. Why? Why do you ask that question?" It was as though he suspected a trick.

"In investigations such as this one," Rogers explained half-humorously, "seemingly irrelevant questions may be asked."

"May I put in my say, Mr. Plummer?" Douglas Kramer spoke up for the first time since he had offered his alibi.

"Yes, of course."

"The subject of inheritance was up a moment ago, and the part it might play in establishing a motive for Mr. Fulton's death."

"Yes?"

"Well, it's like this. I happen to be a lawyer, junior partner, in fact, in the law firm that handled all of Mr. Fulton's legal business. I'm not familiar with all of it. I'm not old enough for that, because he's been lawing for a couple of generations, I believe. But that's not the point. What I want to say is that I drew his will for him only a few weeks ago—"

"Did you, really?" Miss Forbes was eager; there was a glitter of anticipation in her dark eyes.

"Yes."

"What—? Well—sorry I interrupted."

Plummer broke into the pause that followed this odd outburst. "What were you going to tell us, Mr. Kramer?"

"Ordinarily an attorney would keep still. But this is an extraordinary circumstance. The client is dead, and it's only a matter of a short time until the will is made public. I have no hesitancy, therefore, in helping you in your investigation. In so far as Miss Forbes and Mrs. DeWitt are concerned——"

"Tell me quickly," urged Mrs. DeWitt, leaning in her eagerness toward Kramer across the glowing coals of the campfire.

"Both you and Miss Forbes are mentioned in the will," Kramer went on, exasperatingly slow and deliberate of manner. "Mentioned handsomely, in fact. It's a matter of percentages, of course. After debts and several large charities, the residue is divided among the heirs, children by both marriages getting by far the larger percentage, although nieces and nephews are remembered substantially ——all depending, of course, upon what remains after liquidation and federal and state taxes."

"Thank God for that," breathed Miss Forbes with feeling.

"But you got a motive now, Miss Forbes," Hammond reminded her.

"I don't mind that, old boy, just so I get the money."

17

CLAUDIA BENSON experienced a definite feeling of distaste for Miss Forbes. The fact that her uncle had died by the hand of a murderer appeared to mean nothing; her only interest was in what might be coming to her under the will of the old man whose body now lay in one of the tents back in the dark shadows.

Ben Mayfield threw several sticks of wood upon the embers and they blazed up in a flash of warm, yellow flames. This cheerful note in the gloomy setting was welcome. Sleep was gone from Claudia's eyes. As long as she sat quietly the weariness in her muscles didn't trouble her. Miss Forbes seemed to have thrown off a great burden, as if years had rolled off her shoulders. Al DeWitt and his wife had both assumed an air of expansive indulgence toward the other hikers; they appeared to have no worries, no troubles. Not even the fact that there now had been established significant motives in the death of the old man meant anything to them. Al DeWitt crossed his legs and cocked his head in the direction of the chief ranger.

"What's a motive now in the old gentleman's death, Mr. Plummer, when you take into consideration that other killing back at Merced Lake? If the same fellow killed both Hodges and Fulton? I never saw Hodges before in all my life until last Monday morning when we all hit the trail together."

"And I don't go about killing miscellaneous gentlemen,

either, Mr. Plummer," said Miss Forbes with a derisive chuckle.

"I'll admit quite frankly," Plummer answered soberly, "that what is a perfectly good motive in the death of Mr. Fulton won't furnish a motive in the Hodges murder. Unless——" he took hold of the stiff brim of his hat and set it tighter on his head—"unless Hodges died of a mistake."

"A mistake?" echoed Hammond. "That's just the trouble. What if there's another mistake? And I'm it?"

"Let's not be funny about this business," chided Beryl Lindsay.

"When I say mistake," Plummer took up calmly, "I mean mistake. The person who killed Mr. Fulton probably thought he was killing the old gentleman at Merced Lake, although the man he actually killed was Hodges."

"Yeah?" objected DeWitt lightly, "that's stretching it just a bit too far, Mr. Plummer. One motive, one crime is what I say. Now if I killed the old man so May could inherit—mind you, it's hypothetical; I'm just supposing—wouldn't you think I'd make awfully sure of it before I did it?"

"I suppose you would," Plummer agreed. "But suppose that at the time you didn't know that Mr. Hodges and Mr. Fulton had changed tents? That happened, you remember."

An uneasy stir ran like a ripple of foreboding through the hikers about the campfire. Al DeWitt suddenly uncrossed his legs and recrossed them. His wife drew her sweater closer about her throat as if she felt a draft, although there was no air stirring. Leon Mullins cleared his throat and coughed quietly.

"Yes, I remember it was brought out at Merced Lake,"

DeWitt said.

"Did you know about it before that?"

"No, sir."

"Whatever became of the knife that killed Hodges?" asked Frederick Dudley in the heavy silence that followed.

"It's still missing," asserted Bruce Milbank. The naturalist had sat slumped in his chair, his dark brown boots thrust toward the fire. He had appeared to be dozing, his hat over his face. He straightened up and looked at the chief ranger.

"Although it was not the cause of Mr. Fulton's death, we'd like very much to know what became of that knife," Plummer stated as if he expected someone to produce it promptly.

"I was unjustly accused of having it at Merced Lake. After the crime," Dudley remarked in an aggrieved tone. "I don't think the boy back there should have made such an unsupported statement in so serious a matter. Like Mr. DeWitt, who claims he had never seen the man prior to last Monday, I'd never so much as heard of him up to that time. As for killing anybody, that's out. Why, I've never even been arrested in my whole life; one traffic ticket— one, mind you—is the extent of my criminal record."

"The boy could have been mistaken," Plummer agreed.

"He *was* mistaken," Dudley's voice rang with emphasis.

"I believe you, Mr. Dudley," said Beryl Lindsay in instant approval, as if he had meant the denial for her ears alone.

The earnestness of her response excited a small wave of amusement which washed along the circle about the campfire. For a moment the school teacher was unaware that she was the cause of it, and then when she discovered the fact, she became slightly indignant. "There's such a thing as moral righteousness; it was in every fiber of Mr. Dudley's being when he said that about the knife," she said defiantly.

"Thank you, Miss Lindsay," Dudley said gravely.

"Yes, but who's guilty?" Hammond rudely interrupted this exchange of amenities. "That's the main thing. If it's going to take us two days more to hike out of this back country, I want to be able to do it without having my throat slit."

"The mills of the gods grind slowly," said Turley grimly, striking a match on the sole of his boot and lighting his pipe. He tossed the match stick upon the fire and watched it flash up.

"Just so they don't stop grinding," remarked Ralph Stoner, who had sat as if fascinated by the conversation.

"But what I want to know, and it's still not even been mentioned except by me, is about the leaf torn out of my notebook," Beryl Lindsay suddenly was off. "It's little things that mean so much in cases like this. I could cite you case after case that I've heard about where just the flimsiest little scrap of nothing at all has unraveled the whole mystery. Now somebody down at Merced Lake that morning when Mr. Plummer held the first inquiry tore half a page out of a perfectly good notebook I'd bought especially for this trip. It isn't the damage to my notebook; that's not a killing matter. But why was it done?" She looked about the circle as if daring anybody to dispute the importance of the point.

"If somebody had wanted the paper to write on," she continued, "that is, just to jot down any old memorandum —he would have asked for it. But if it was something

undercover, it would be done just the way it was done—
without asking. Now, why can't we start on that lead?"

William Turley took his pipe from between his lips
and turned to the school teacher two chairs removed from
his own. He pointed at her with his pipe stem.

"Now, that's something, Miss Lindsay—"

"You were going to call me Beryl, and I was to call
you Bill."

"All right—Beryl." Turley smiled self-consciously. "As
I was about to say, that matter is something I didn't dream
would come up for discussion. I've kept still because I
hadn't seen it in the light in which you just put it. I saw
it happen—"

"You?" exclaimed Miss Lindsay.

"The person didn't make any secret of it at the time.
Did it quite openly, in fact. Wrote something on the piece
of paper and—here's the interesting part—went over to
Milbank's coat which was hanging on a tree and slipped
it into a pocket."

"Tell us who it was," urged May DeWitt, leaning forward eagerly.

"Well—one sometimes sees things that he doesn't ordinarily say anything about. It happens that it was a young
lady—"

"A young lady!"

Claudia was aware that many eyes were turning in
curiosity upon her, and she felt a sudden slight embarrassment.

"Yes. You see," Turley continued, "I regarded it at
the moment as nothing more than a bit of sentiment upon
the part of a romantic young person whose attentions

had become focused upon a good-looking forest ranger."

Claudia suddenly seethed with anger, for all eyes were staring at her, and many lips were parted in smiles of understanding. She sprang to her feet in hot denial.

"It wasn't I!" she exclaimed. "I wouldn't do any such thing!"

"My dear young lady," Turley began with abject apology in his voice. "I didn't say it was you. I didn't mean even to imply that it was you. I'm speaking of the other young lady—the radio singer who deserted us at Tuolumne Meadows."

Claudia sat down in confusion, but thankful that the matter had been so quickly corrected. Beryl Lindsay leaned over and patted her on the knee, then she straightened up and directed her attention mischievously to Bruce Milbank.

"I think Bruce ought to be made to read us the note. Or, at least, tell us whether Miss Sherman writes a hot love letter—or the platonic type."

"Just a minute, everybody." Bruce Milbank sat suddenly upright and in the firelight his face darkened with the blood that surged into his cheeks. "That love note, as you call it, was something else again—"

"Excuse me, Bruce," interrupted Rogers quietly, and the naturalist promptly retired from the field. Rogers turned to the others of the circle. "The note in question," he explained, "has been something of a puzzle. I think Bruce had it simmered down to one or two, or possibly three, persons who might have written it. Miss Sherman was one of them. It wasn't a love note in any sense. It contained a shrewd observation, the truth of which, however, is yet to be demonstrated. Miss Sherman had harked back to her Shakespeare."

"Shakespeare? What's he got to do with it?" asked Hammond.

"You wouldn't understand it, dumb brain," jeered DeWitt.

"Oh, I wouldn't, wouldn't I?"

"Let's hear what it is." Miss Lindsay was impatient. "Go on, Professor Rogers, tell us."

"You recall Lady Macbeth's sleep-walking scene after the murder. In fancy her hands are stained with blood; it clings, it is indelible, nothing can remove the spot. She washes her hand again and again to no avail. Well, what Miss Sherman wrote in her note was this: 'One of the party washes his hands so frequently. Why?'"

Silence fell on the group when Rogers ceased. There were furtive glances as suspicion went hunting for a victim.

"Oh, then that's why you asked that perfectly crazy question on the way down from Vogelsang," exclaimed Miss Lindsay. "You wanted to know if I'd seen anybody washing his hands. And I told you— Oh, my goodness, what have I done? Mr. Mullins! I said Mr. Mullins had washed his hands a lot. I was going to try to see if he was still doing it. But—Mr. Mullins!" She turned in consternation to the cowboy who sat leaning forward, elbows on knees, staring into the fire. The broad brim of his huge hat threw his face in complete shadow. He sat as if carved of stone, the flickering firelight throwing fantastic shadows about his hunched shoulders. But as the eyes of the group fastened firmly upon him it was plain that he sat tense and quivering, as if every muscle was strained to the breaking point. Suddenly he sat back and faced Rogers.

"Well, what of it? I've always washed my hands a lot,

because I like to keep clean. But I don't wash 'em any oftener than you other folks, do I?" His voice was slightly ragged.

"Do you? Or did you at Merced Lake, and for a day or two after that?" asked Plummer.

"I don't know." He sparred for time, the muscles of his face contracted in a fierce effort at recollection. "Maybe I did. But I don't recall any reason why I should."

"But you did," insisted Beryl Lindsay. "I saw you washing your hands several times. Once right after you'd got through doing it you did it again."

"Well, Miss Lindsay, I'm not going to dispute a lady. If you say I did, I guess I did, but I wouldn't be conscious of doing it, would I?" It seemed to be an appeal for forbearance. "I don't see anything wrong with it."

"Now, Mr. Mullins," Rogers interrupted, "let's go back to the Merced Lake affair. You knew Harry Hodges, didn't you? You knew him when his name was Harry Britain."

"Yes, I knew him then." Mullins looked oddly at Miss Forbes. "But I don't know what that has to do with it."

"You once had some trouble with the man. He absconded with money that belonged to you. In South America. And with your wife."

"He did that, yes."

"It provides an excellent motive for his murder, say, if you had held it against him, as you must have done—"

"Now, I didn't kill him!" Mullins interrupted. "I'll admit that at times in the past I thought of it. But I got over it. We were friends at the last, just as we had been at the beginning years ago. I'd forgiven him. That's why—"

"That's why what?" Rogers pressed, after a moment's silence.

"Nothing."

"You were in the murdered man's tent alone that morning. You've admitted that. You said you went in just to look at him. Now, didn't you——?"

"Didn't I what?" Mullins spoke with a show of decreasing resistance to Rogers' attack. "I—— Yes, I went in to see Harry. I told you that. I told you that I couldn't see much but that knife sticking in his heart. It was the biggest thing in the tent. It was all I could see. I couldn't look anywhere without seeing it."

"And you——" Rogers' tone was persuasive.

"All right, all right," Mullins said suddenly, "I pulled the knife out. I had to do it. I couldn't bear to see it sticking there. I threw it out on the ground——"

"After you'd cleaned it?"

"Yes. I guess so. I don't know why I did that, though. I used my handkerchief, then threw it away. I got some blood on my hands, and had to wash it off——" He stopped with an odd look on his face, then went on: "It seemed that I just couldn't get it all off. No matter how much I washed. I couldn't eat knowing maybe some of it was still on." He looked startled. "But I didn't kill him. Honest to God I didn't kill Harry."

"All right," said Plummer, "you say you didn't do it."

"I didn't. I tell you, I didn't."

18

CHIEF RANGER FLOYD PLUMMER was puzzled. He had had several hard nuts to crack in the years he had been in Yosemite, but nothing that approached in toughness the present one. Two members of the seven-day hiking party had died at the hands of an unknown slayer and after all their questioning, both his own and that of Professor Huntoon Rogers, they seemed no nearer to a solution than they had been that first morning at Merced Lake. They had uncovered the essential facts, but that was about all it amounted to so far. Nothing they had learned warranted an arrest, much less the bringing before the resident commissioner at government center of anyone charged with murder. And, what was more, he couldn't make out Rogers.

Rogers leaned forward and once again picked up the small bunch of keys on the table and examined them. In the silence that had settled upon the camp there came the steady rushing sound of the White Cascade. Bruce Milbank yawned. Bruce had had a hard day of it; he ought to be in bed. The others had now gone to their tents. The session about the campfire had been a long one, and everybody had been thoroughly tired out.

"You're not going to make a green monkey out of those keys, Hunt," the chief ranger remarked.

Rogers laid them down among the other articles on the table. They were the things that old Thomas Fulton had carried in his pockets, as well as the articles that had made up his pack. The lot of them had been put aside earlier for examination when the hikers should have gone to bed. The trio had waited until Mayfield had assured them that they would be undisturbed in the dining room and Mayfield had gone off to bed himself on the promise that they would put out the light when they had finished.

"Unfortunately not," Rogers said at length.

Plummer wondered what there was about an elusive jade monkey that so absorbed Rogers' thoughts. The maid's word down at the hotel was the only assurance they had that the thing even existed. And even so, the old man probably had stowed it away somewhere in his room before he left for the hike. They hadn't really searched for the thing last night when they looked for it, not a thorough search, at any rate. And if the maid was correct in her suspicions that someone had visited the room that morning after the old man left for Happy Isles, then in all probability it had been stolen. And so, why? Rogers spoke again.

"It seems important for just one reason, Floyd. The fact that Hugh Buckingham gave it to the old gentleman. The old gentleman is dead, and so, very likely, is Buckingham."

"What could it signify? I mean, why would that be important?"

"That's what I am trying to figure out." Rogers' manner was thoughtful as he stared into the shadowy corners of the room. "Just now there seems to be no possible connection. I don't know how the jade monkey could mean anything at all—but it's in the picture. Do you know anything about carrier pigeons?"

"Carrier pigeons? No."

"Their use in war time? Buckingham had been a fancier of carriers. In your various conversations with Fulton did he ever mention pigeons?"

"No." Plummer was completely mystified.

"That's too long a story to go into tonight," Rogers remarked. "It's getting late." He turned to Milbank. "We searched the ground carefully where the old man's body was found, didn't we?"

"As carefully as could be done, sir." Milbank leaned forward with elbows on the table. "Why don't we make an announcement tomorrow about this green monkey? Say it's missing, and ask the hikers to keep an eye out for it?"

"No!" Rogers' tone was emphatic. Milbank opened his tired eyes wider. He murmured an apology and Rogers went on. "Suppose it figures in the murder? Suppose the murderer already has killed two men to get his hands on it, what then? In that case we'd never find it, or discover its significance. Moreover, if we can manage to learn who has it in his possession, isn't that fact of possession a strong indication of guilt?" Rogers halted and rubbed the side of his large nose thoughtfully. "I'm merely thinking aloud," he explained. "That's one line of reasoning. The motive of the two crimes is possession of the piece of jade, although for exactly what reason is not yet clear. On the other hand we have established a very strong motive for the death of Mr. Fulton—avarice, greed, impatience over the long waiting for a possible inheritance. A very excellent motive indeed for three persons—the two De-Witts and Miss Forbes. Of these three Al DeWitt, being the man, is the logical suspect in the murder of Mr. Fulton, although it is not too much for a woman to have done. If the death of Harry Hodges was an accident murder, that

could fit in with DeWitt or either of the two women."
Rogers paused and smiled.

"Go on," urged Plummer.

"If you both weren't members of the park service I
wouldn't be thinking aloud like this."

"Don't worry about anything you may say getting out
to the others. Go on with your thinking aloud, please."

"On the other hand, Mullins has gone so far as to admit
that he removed the knife from Hodges' body. Under
pressure would he go further and admit that he also drove
the knife into Hodges' body? These admissions frequently
are in reality half steps to full confession of guilt. Mullins
has a motive, if you discard his assertion of renewed
friendship for the man who once stole his money and his
wife.

"But—if he killed Hodges for that reason, why murder
poor old Mr. Fulton? Fulton's death in that event couldn't
be an accident murder, for the murderer already has accomplished his purpose in the first death. The next question, then, is, did Mr. Fulton know too much about the
death of Hodges, and Mullins, say, in fear of discovery
had to do away with him?"

"I can't believe that, Professor," Milbank said. "It's
been several days now since Hodges died. I've seen the old
man every day since, walked miles with him alone, talked
with him. He didn't have anything like that on his mind;
he didn't act like he was concealing anything. He was a
blunt, outspoken old gentleman, and if he knew anything
about Hodges' death I'm pretty sure he would have come
out with it at some time in the last few days."

"Well, there you have another puzzling angle," Rogers
resumed his analysis. "If Mullins killed Hodges, why,

then, would he kill Fulton? If Mullins were to inherit something, say, from the old man, or benefit in some way, then you'd hook him up to the death of Fulton very easily. Although—and here's a point—a murderer seldom kills one man for a particular reason and another man for an entirely different and unrelated motive. Multiple killings almost invariably result from related motives. If Mullins supposedly had a reason for killing Fulton, then the death of Hodges might still be an accident killing in his case. There could be two explanations of the Hodges death, accident or the original motive of an old hatred—if Mullins had any reason for killing Fulton. But he hasn't.

"And so I come back to the jade monkey." Rogers smiled faintly. "The fact that Hugh Buckingham gave it to Mr. Fulton, and the further fact that both of them are now dead—assuming that the body found in Lost Valley is Buckingham's—must add up to something."

"Well, then, Professor," said Milbank, now wide awake, "the fellow you maybe are looking for actually has killed three people."

"That's right, Hunt," agreed Plummer with suppressed excitement.

"I realize that fact. Perhaps we can solve all of Yosemite's puzzles at one blow. But if it turns out that Mr. Fulton was killed for his money, then where does that leave us—and Superintendent Haverly down on the Valley floor who's worrying about that Lost Valley body?"

"It gets more and more tangled, doesn't it?" said Milbank with a note of concern in his voice. "What do we do, Mr. Plummer—carry on tomorrow to May Lake, and Valley floor next day after?"

"It's the only thing you can do, Bruce. You've got some

dyed-in-the-wool hikers in this bunch. Miss Lindsay, for instance, Miss Benson, and the men, except for Al DeWitt. That fellow's got me puzzled. The rest of the crowd seems to be tough-fibered mentally as well as physically. Miss Sherman dropped out, of course—"

"It was blisters, Mr. Plummer. Nothing else but blisters. I got fed up taping them for her. You don't suppose she knows anything about the killings?" he turned to Rogers.

"She produced an interesting clue. I assume it was purely one of observation. She couldn't have had a hand in the death of Mr. Fulton, of course. And, therefore, probably knows nothing about the Hodges death. I suppose there would be no trouble getting in touch with her if we needed her later, Floyd?"

"We keep a file of the reservations for this hike. Her address would be there."

"Well, is anybody thinking of going to bed tonight?" Milbank yawned. "For once I'll admit I've had a day of it."

Rogers stirred about among the articles that had belonged to the dead man. He turned through the miscellaneous objects, discarding them one by one, shoving them toward the chief ranger, who was preparing to do them into a bundle.

"No green monkey?" Plummer inquired lightly.

"Not even any kind of monkey," he said with a twinkle in his eyes. "I hope the thing won't make a monkey out of me before I get through with it."

"All set?" Plummer stood ready to extinguish the light.

"Turn it out," said Milbank from the ground outside. Rogers went down the steps. The light blacked out, and

Plummer's cautious footsteps came down upon the gravel beside them. Milbank snapped on his flashlight and the three started toward the dormitory tent.

A formless blob suddenly confronted them in the darkness. Plummer halted instantly with a word of caution to the other two.

"It's me, Stoner," said a voice, as Milbank flashed his light upon the man.

"What's going on?" asked Plummer.

"Oh—nothing in particular," Stoner replied quietly. "I was just a bit curious about Mullins, so I came out to look him up."

"What about him?"

"He sneaked out of the dormitory tent about half an hour ago, and didn't come back. I got to thinking that maybe he might have got into trouble."

"What kind of trouble?"

"He thought I was asleep, I guess. The others certainly were all hard at it. I noticed he only took off his shoes when he rolled in. That was funny, and so I couldn't get to sleep."

"Probably went to the washroom." Plummer was unconcerned.

"I looked there first. He wouldn't be hiking out, would he?"

"I don't know," Plummer answered quietly. "Why would he?"

"Well, from what was said tonight about his taking the knife out of Hodges' body, it doesn't take much imagination to guess maybe the whole story hasn't been told yet."

"Is that the way it struck you?" Plummer asked.

"It sure did. You don't suppose he got to thinking things

over, and decided to pull out?"

"He'd have to be a better woodsman than I think he is to hike anywhere in the dark. Bruce or I probably could follow the trail back to Tuolumne Meadows, but I don't think he could."

"Maybe he just got away far enough tonight to be safe and plans to go on after it's light enough to see."

"He won't get far." Plummer's voice was sober.

"But what if he's just strolled out because he couldn't sleep after what's been told, and has fallen and hurt himself?"

"You would bring that up," said Milbank wearily. He meant it to be humorous.

"But we ought to look him up, don't you think?"

"I'm afraid so."

"I'll rout the others out." Stoner suddenly was all energy.

"Hold it." Plummer spoke sharply but quietly. "The four of us are enough."

"All right. Which way do we start looking?"

They paired off, Plummer and Rogers together, and Stoner with Milbank. They searched through the camp grounds and met again at the fire, whose dying embers now made only a ghostly light on the ground.

Plummer's voice held a note of irritation. "On the theory that he might have fallen and hurt himself near camp it's no go. If he wandered farther just to think things over and managed to get into trouble, which way would he go? What do you think, Bruce?"

"He wouldn't go down toward Waterwheel Falls, and I don't think he'd go up Cold Canyon trail."

"That leaves Tuolumne Meadows or May Lake."

"But if it was just to think things over, say, wouldn't he go back over the Tuolumne Meadows trail, which he knows, rather than a trail he hasn't been on?"

"That's right. Also, if he's taking French leave, it would be Tuolumne Meadows where he might thumb a ride on the Tioga Road. He's a fool, though, to do that, because we can stop him anywhere by telephoning the boys at the checking stations." He paused and the river filled in the silence. "Well, let's go up the Tuolumne trail a little way, and see what we can find."

They set off in the darkness, their flashlights picking out the rough ground of the trail. Plummer was weary to the marrow of his bones, and he knew that Milbank, a younger man, must be near exhaustion. Milbank hadn't spoken for a long while, and he stumbled frequently. Rogers seemed to call upon unused sources of energy. Apparently he regarded the whole affair lightly; the possibility that Mullins was attempting an escape made little impression. Plummer wondered if Rogers believed the solution was simpler than that.

They back-tracked on the Tuolumne Meadows trail for at least a mile before they gave it up as a bad job. Repeatedly they stopped and called Mullins' name. Stoner all the while appeared to regret his part in the night's adventure, but in order to prove that there was no hoax he urged them at the end of it into the dormitory tent.

"Take a look at his bed. You'll see he was there. The imprint of his body's there, but he ain't."

Plummer turned his flashlight on the narrow bed. It was empty as Stoner had asserted it would be. The chief ranger was puzzled. All four of them, though, got to bed in the dark to a creaking of springs, and a threshing of the blankets, and Plummer fell asleep planning how he would telephone in the morning to cut off any escape if Mullins was attempting to leave the park, and then organize searching parties to beat the trails about Glen Aulin.

19

CLAUDIA BENSON wakened when the gray light of dawn was making a dim rectangle of the dormitory tent roof over her head. Birds were beginning to waken, a squirrel was rustling somewhere, or perhaps it was a deer wandering through camp. The air was chilly, for the altitude was nearly eight thousand feet, and near-by peaks were snow-capped. She lay in her warm blankets and with eyes wide open thought soberly of the many things that had happened since they left Happy Isles.

Beryl Lindsay was still asleep, a dark mound of blankets two beds away. There were only the two of them in the tent. At Tuolumne Meadows there had been four, but Ruth Sherman had quit the party, and Miss Forbes had decided at dinner time last night to move into a private tent. Claudia had felt safer sleeping with the other women after her experience alone at Vogelsang. There was something very practical about Beryl Lindsay, something earthy which she liked. If she were strayed in the wilderness she'd rather that it were in company with Beryl Lindsay than with anybody else; they'd make out together. But how did the woman do so much hiking, whence all the terrific energy in a body that seemed to be over-fat?

As Claudia lay thinking, Beryl Lindsay threw aside her blankets with a mighty heave, drew on a dressing gown and, apparently assuming that Claudia still slept, went outside to the washroom. Claudia was still lazily resting when the school teacher came back, struck a match, and dropped it into the small sheet iron stove. Obviously Beryl Lindsay now labored under some curious excitement. She hadn't said a word, but Claudia could sense an odd perturbation in her manner and she wondered what could have happened.

"Good morning, Beryl," said Claudia, deciding to get up.

"Oh, did I wake you up, dear? I'm sorry."

"I've been awake for a long time."

"Sleep well?"

"Like a log. In spite of everything."

"So did I."

Claudia got up and with utmost speed because of the chill air got into her hiking clothes. She wondered what it was that so agitated her tent mate.

"The sun's up, of course," said the school teacher, "but down here in the canyon you wouldn't know it, would you?"

"No."

"It's surprisingly light outside, although it doesn't look it from inside this tent."

"Any deer in camp this morning?"

"No—that wasn't what I saw."

"What did you see?"

Beryl Lindsay appeared startled, as if she had disclosed something against her better judgment.

"Nothing," she said, absorbed in her sketchy makeup before the dim little glass on the dresser.

"You're awfully mysterious this morning about something, Beryl."

"I've always found it the best policy not to say too much, or better still, nothing at all, unless I'm absolutely sure of what I know. Even then it's not always best to talk about it. One can be so awfully wrong. But I was never so shocked in my life."

"Well," laughed Claudia, "whenever you decide to tell me I suppose I'll listen." She ended rather weakly, for she had always prided herself on not showing any curiosity, and here she was being as curious as a girl of fourteen over something that did not concern her.

"I'll see you at breakfast, dear," said Miss Lindsay, giving a final touch to the red and yellow scarf about her head in a rush to leave. "I want to take one more look at the cascade before we say good-bye to this camp. In spite of what's happened, I think I like this place best of any we've seen. So long. See you at breakfast."

She hurried away without giving Claudia time to suggest that in a few more minutes she could join her. It was mystifying. Claudia wondered if Beryl Lindsay was embarrassed. That's what it seemed like. The school teacher's footsteps died away on the hard ground outside, and Claudia, now that the little sheet iron stove had begun to heat up the interior of the dormitory, settled down to a leisurely attention to her makeup. Someone went by outside. Claudia heard voices and recognized Mrs. DeWitt and Mr. Turley. Their paths seemed to have met just outside.

"What was the row going on in camp last night?"

"I don't know. I didn't hear any." Turley's voice held a tone of amusement.

"You certainly must be a sound sleeper with a clear conscience."

"I am—and have. What did you hear?"

"I thought they must surely wake everybody up, walking around back in here among the tents. They had flash-lights. Later I heard them calling to somebody."

"When was that?"

"Sometime early last night."

"Who was looking for whom?"

"I didn't hear distinctly. It wasn't you, was it?"

"Not me," chuckled Turley. "Oh, now that you speak of it, I do remember that some of the fellows came in late last night. I just barely waked up, then dropped off to sleep again. I'm the second one up in our tent this morning. Mullins is up and away somewhere already. The others are still dead to the world, except Dudley. He showed signs of life just as I was leaving."

Apparently the two walked away together, for their voices grew faint and the sound of their footsteps was lost against the tumbling roar of the cascade. Claudia finished her toilet, got together her few belongings, did them up in a pack and buckled the strap, for the party would be leaving after breakfast for May Lake. She slung the pack over her shoulder and went outside into the fresh, cold air. She walked leisurely with hands in pockets toward the central tent, where already there were signs of break-fast in the curling blue smoke from the kitchen range. She put her pack down upon a chair near the ashes of last night's fire and wondered what to do. As she stood there, Miss Forbes came along the trail from below. She was swinging her stick, her head bowed as if she was absorbed in her thoughts.

"You're out early this morning," said Claudia.

"I like to get up early. I've already had a little stroll." She indicated the trail along the Tuolumne. "It's lovely at this time of day. I saw a fawn hidden away in a tiny little dell—"

"Did you touch it?" asked Claudia in alarm.

"No, I didn't. I know that one mustn't do that. The doe, they say, detects the odor of the human hand and will abandon her fawn. No, I was very careful. The tiny thing lay very still, not moving a muscle, or even blinking."

Miss Forbes put her cigarette between her lips, drew a long breath, then dropped the stub on the ground and stepped on it. Something that Claudia saw in the movement of the graceful hand made her blink. Heretofore she hadn't noticed any rings on Miss Forbes' fingers at any time on the trip, but now there was a small gold band upon the third finger of the left hand. She made no effort at concealing the fact, and Claudia offered no comment. Nor did she give any sign that she had noticed it.

"I suppose we'll go on as usual after breakfast," said Claudia.

"Yes, I think so. There was no intimation to the contrary last night. Poor old Uncle Tom though—the party will miss him. And he did seem to be enjoying the hike. I suppose that as a group we'll just go on, and that the park service will bring in a pack mule. They did that down at Merced Lake."

Miss Forbes was very calm, even detached and unfeeling about her uncle's death; it was as if he had been somebody not even remotely connected with her own private life.

"They telephoned, you know, after they brought the body up to camp. I heard something about a pack horse," Claudia offered.

"I heard that too."

Several hikers arrived together from the tents hungrily

intent upon breakfast. Jack Hammond opened the door to the dining room, then backed out and shook his head. The DeWitts arrived, followed by Frederick Dudley. Turley wandered in from the direction of the cascade and with him was Beryl Lindsay. Breakfast was announced, and the party made a good natured rush into the dining room where bacon and eggs already were upon the table. Rogers, accompanied by the chief ranger and Bruce Milbank, brought up the rear, and Miss Forbes as usual managed to find a chair between Rogers and Plummer.

Claudia as she looked about the table noted a vacant chair. With a start she realized that somebody was missing.

"Why, where's Mr. Mullins this morning?" inquired Mrs. DeWitt.

There was a short silence, a swift exchange of glances, and the chief ranger coughed. Ralph Stoner was on the point of saying something when Miss Forbes remarked:

"Oh, he'll be along soon."

"Do you mean that you've seen him?" Bruce Milbank stared slightly at Miss Forbes, who was salting her egg.

"I've noticed that he hasn't missed a meal since we started."

"Yes, but——"

"But this time it's different." Stoner was eager to tell what he knew. "Do you know what happened last night, Miss Forbes? Four of us hunted all over camp for the guy, and we couldn't find him."

"I saw him this morning," said Beryl Lindsay, curiously precise.

"Then he really came back?" Milbank seemed greatly relieved.

Claudia did not understand the exchange of glances

between the chief ranger and Bruce Milbank. Stoner sat
with mouth partly open. Rogers' eyes were twinkling at
this development.

"If he went away—" Miss Lindsay's voice had a
skeptical note in it. "I hope I'm not asked to tell you
where I saw him this morning." Her broad face slowly
reddened with embarrassment. She stammered. "I was
shocked."

"I would expect you to be," observed Miss Forbes in
a matter-of-fact tone meant to embarrass further the
blushing teacher.

"I'm not saying anything more." Beryl Lindsay's voice
was less expressive than her burning cheeks. "You explain
it. I can't. As I say, I was shocked. I didn't suppose the
park service would countenance any such thing—"

"Now, just a minute, ladies, please," the chief ranger
plunged intrepidly into the argument. "Just a minute. And
we'll find out what this is all about. First, let me say that
Mr. Mullins disappeared last night from the men's dormitory, and Bruce and Stoner and Rogers helped me hunt
him. Without success. We'd already had a hard day, as
you know. And now, Miss Lindsay—" he turned to the
school teacher—"you say you saw something that shocked
you—"

"I did! Mr. Mullins came out of Miss Forbes' tent!"
Her voice was vibrant with indignation.

"Well—" the chief ranger coughed behind his hand
and looked at Miss Forbes, who seemed oblivious of the
charge as she continued slowly to butter a piece of toast.
"Perhaps there's an explanation—"

"The explanation is very simple," was the casual reply.
Claudia noted again the narrow gold band upon her left

hand. "In private life I'm Mrs. Leon Mullins. Professionally, as a sculptress, I prefer to be called Miss Forbes." The wedding ring seemed to Claudia to be just a trifle more prominent on her finger than it had been. Perhaps it was the way Miss Forbes managed to hold her hand so that all at the table might see.

"But——" exploded Beryl Lindsay in consternation.

"Yes, I know, you're more shocked than ever now, aren't you? I'll accept your apology, although I don't know why I should."

"Yes, I know, but——" Beryl Lindsay was like a terrier worrying at a rat hole.

Miss Forbes' face suddenly darkened; her lips thinned a trifle and her eyes fired up.

"Still you don't want to believe it!" She put down her knife suddenly, tore open the zipper of her purse, fumbled about for a moment among its contents, and drew out the photostat of her driver's license in a transparent case. "Pass it to the lady," she said coldly to Plummer. "She'll believe this, perhaps. It's made out to Mrs. Maribel Forbes Mullins."

The license was passed along to Beryl Lindsay, who refused to touch it. "That's my point. I'm not doubting your word, my dear Mrs. Mullins. But there are conventions——"

"Are there?" Miss Forbes inquired indifferently. "I've never been much concerned with them." Her voice had resumed its level of casualness.

"But, Mrs. Mullins," Rogers said quietly.

"Yes?"

"There must be some explanation. You had a reason for starting on this hike as Miss Forbes, and then deciding to finish it as Mrs. Mullins. If I had any curiosity in the matter at all, it would be to know why you did it. Does it by chance have any connection with what happened here yesterday?"

"Yes, Professor, it does." Miss Forbes addressed her remarks entirely to Rogers, as if it were no concern of the others. Her voice dropped slightly so that some who listened were obliged to strain to hear. "Uncle Tom is dead. That's the whole explanation."

Miss Forbes neglected her breakfast now. "You see," she went on, "Uncle Tom never approved of my marital adventures. They've been rather many, and somewhat complicated. A young girl doesn't have much sense about such things as marriage. At least I didn't. I just married, and got divorced, and married again—you know how some of us women do. Well, that was it, and Uncle Tom didn't approve. That's why he cut me out of his will. And then, after I finally settled down and applied myself to sculpture, he was inclined to forget my checkered past.

"But now, here's the point. Leon and I were married down in Mexico last Christmas, and I was pretty sure that Uncle Tom hadn't heard about it, and so until I could sound him out on how he felt about still another marriage, I didn't want to complicate things by acknowledging a new husband, not when an inheritance was at stake. I wanted to get him used to the idea before I sprang Leon on him. I didn't want to revive old prejudices, you understand.

"And why didn't I leave Leon at Camp Curry? Well, Leon likes this sort of thing, so why shouldn't he come along? We could play a harmless little game of deception until we knew how the old man would take it. But—Uncle

Tom is dead, and there's no further point in keeping the thing dark."

The sound of approaching footsteps on the gravel outside the door interrupted. The door was seized and pulled quickly open.

"Here's Leon now," Miss Forbes said. Then lifting her voice, she called out: "Come on in, Leon. You're the man of the hour."

20

CHIEF RANGER PLUMMER lengthened his stride and set out in pursuit of Huntoon Rogers, who had already disappeared from view on the trail. The main party under Bruce Milbank's guidance had been gone from Glen Aulin for more than an hour. Rogers and Plummer had waited for the pack mule from Tuolumne Meadows. The blanketed body of old Mr. Fulton had been lashed to the mule's back and the rangers had taken the trail to the meadows where a truck waited to carry it down the Tioga Road to the Valley floor.

This business of murder in Yosemite had got very much under the chief ranger's skin. Yosemite was a playground, a region of natural wonders dedicated to the recreation of a people; murder in Yosemite was nothing short of profanation. The men of the park service worked hard to keep the area as Nature intended it to be. But already he'd spent the greater part of a week trying to solve the murder of Harry Hodges, and now the problem of old man Fulton's death had been dumped upon him. Moreover, there was that other puzzle of the body of the man found in Lost Valley.

Although he had had the assistance of Huntoon Rogers, who had been extraordinarily successful as an amateur criminologist, still he wasn't getting anywhere. Somewhere up ahead, in the party that Bruce Milbank was conducting, walked the person who had killed Hodges and Fulton. That was certain now. But there was only this day and the next before the party broke up on the Valley floor. Something had to happen before then. It would be doubly difficult to run the thing down once the hikers scattered. So far he felt he was not warranted in making an arrest, unless—and that's why he was in a great hurry to overtake Rogers, who seemed annoyingly bent on keeping far ahead of him. Finally Plummer called to him. Rogers' voice came faintly from some distance ahead, and the chief ranger thereupon extended himself.

"Well," he said, when at last he found Rogers sitting comfortably on a log at the side of the trail. "I thought you were trying to run away from me."

"Sit down," Rogers invited. "You're winded."

"Just a little," Plummer admitted, dropping beside his friend. "Is this your idea of a hike?"

"Sorry. Didn't realize I was going so fast."

The chief ranger breathed hard a few times and wiped his face and wrists with his handkerchief. His pack lay on the ground at his feet. A jay alighted in a flash of blue on the branch of a tree near by and raised his dark crest at the pair speculatively. Farther along the trail a woodpecker was methodically inspecting a tree trunk, going round and round as if it were a circular staircase.

"You know," began Plummer when he had got his breath, "that Forbes woman is certainly a hard customer to figure out. What do you make of her?"

"I take 'em as I find 'em. She's a completely self-centered woman with no thought of anything outside her own orbit."

"Now, why couldn't she have announced last night at dinner that she was married to Mullins, and that they'd decided to tent together? Any normal woman under similar circumstances would have done that."

"I agree with you. Any normal woman would."

"No regard for conventions; no thought whatever for what others might think," Plummer complained. "Completely self-centered."

"What do you make of Mullins? He could have said something to the men in the dormitory."

"Yes, he could; that's right. You might argue that the fellow is pretty much under the woman's thumb, or he would have done the decent thing. Miss Lindsay might have had a stroke."

"I don't see how she escaped it."

"But seriously, Hunt, what do you think of Mullins? Does it strike you that he'd take orders from his wife?"

"I wouldn't know, Floyd."

"Do you remember what you said last night about Mullins?"

"Perfectly."

"Well—he's now hooked himself up to old man Fulton. Or rather, she's done it for him. If she has a motive—that motive being to gain an inheritance—then Mullins has it too. The very same motive—tired of waiting for money they're pretty sure will come when the old man dies. And desperate enough to hurry it along."

"That's right."

"Well—is he our man?"

"Have we proved that he killed Hodges?"

"As near as can be proved, I'd think. If he took the knife out of the body, he probably put it in. On the theory that he thought he was killing Fulton. They'd changed tents, you know."

"He's a good candidate, but—"

"But what?"

"Suppose you arrest him for the murder of Hodges and Fulton, and then when he comes to trial you discover that he had an airtight alibi in the Hugh Buckingham murder. We haven't anything to hook him up to that——"

"There you go, Hunt!" The chief ranger was slightly exasperated. "You don't give up once you get your teeth into something. Why should Mullins be hooked up to that crime too? If it is a crime and not a death from natural causes."

"Don't you want all your puzzles solved at one stroke?" Rogers grinned. He got up. "You've got your wind back. What say we jog on? Maybe we'll catch up with the others before they get to May Lake."

The trail led out of the narrow Tuolumne Valley along a stream that had its origin in McGee Lake, and then across high ridges to the night's camp at the foot of Mt. Hoffman.

"I believe I told you that Buckingham was a pigeon fancier," said Rogers as they moved along at a lively pace.

"You've mentioned it. Why?"

"He had a small place in Contra Costa County. Raised pigeons there. Squabs for the market in San Francisco. Had a few carriers too. He once was interested in flying carriers. Carrier pigeons. The queer thing about it is that he went completely out of business after the Japanese attack at Pearl Harbor. Just quit."

The chief ranger thought over these statements as he walked in the wake of Rogers. They didn't seem to make much sense. He remarked as much and after a moment Rogers continued.

"The last Japanese liner that left San Francisco before the Pearl Harbor affair carried away a crate of Buckingham's pigeons. Squabs for the captain's table. Buckingham was in an awful sweat to get them aboard. In fact, sailing was delayed ten minutes, I understand, for Buckingham's squabs."

"Yes," said the chief ranger vaguely, "that's interesting to know, but what bearing does it have on what's happened here?"

The crushing sound of Rogers' heavy boots filled in the silence for a few moments, then he said: "I was just telling you that to see if you could figure out why Mullins, say, would want to kill Buckingham too. It's a far cry from a raiser of squabs in Contra Costa County to a retired millionaire at the Ahwahnee."

"I don't see any connection."

"Buckingham, you know, stayed quite a while at the Ahwahnee."

"I'd forgotten that for the moment."

"And there was a jade monkey in Buckingham's room for a while; later it was in Fulton's room. Sort of a knick-knack. Women are death on those things. Men usually are not so much interested. Maybe that's what makes it important."

"I begin to see what you're driving at, Hunt. Mullins is out of it, in spite of what we've got on him?"

"Not at all. He's still quite a formidable candidate. Maybe, though, we'll have to look for a different motive, one that will embrace all three victims."

"Yes, and maybe we're all wet, Hunt," objected Plummer. "Maybe Mullins killed Hodges because he had once run away with his wife; and maybe DeWitt killed Fulton for the inheritance coming to his wife; and maybe somebody altogether different, Turley, say, or Hammond, or Stoner, just to be naming somebody, killed Buckingham because they were rivals in the squab business—"

"Snap out of it, Floyd," Rogers spoke sharply. "You'll be picking daisies out of the air pretty soon if you let it get you down. Forget it. Let's see if we can overtake the party."

Rogers lengthened the gap between himself and the chief ranger. He drove relentlessly ahead along the trail, setting a pace that a younger man could hardly equal. They came upon McGee Lake but hiked steadily past its blue expanse under a cloudless sky and kept on without sign of slackening. Plummer hadn't hiked like this for several years. He panted for a while in the thin air of eight thousand feet, then got his second wind, and with his pulse thumping inside his head grimly kept the distance of a yard behind Rogers.

"I say," Plummer called out at last, "isn't this enough?"

"I see hikers about half a mile farther on."

They came up with the party on the trail. The hikers were together, sitting about on the rocks in the warm sunshine. Plummer dropped wearily upon a flat rock and tossed his pack upon the ground. Rogers sat down beside Claudia Benson.

"We thought you'd catch up with us before this, Professor. We've been waiting for you."

"Really?"

"Mr. Milbank has been talking about glaciers."

"The pack mule didn't get over to Glen Aulin as early as we had expected."

"Oh."

Turley sat close by. He pulled out his pipe and blew through the stem. He reached into a pocket for his can of tobacco and started to fill his pipe. Only a small quantity, however, poured out, so he shook the can, looked into it, and was about to toss it away when he caught Milbank's eye.

"One doesn't throw empty cans away just anywhere in Yosemite," he said, grinning. "I've learned my lesson on this hike, and I save my trash until I can put it in a trash can."

Milbank commented approvingly and Turley leaned forward and laid hold of the pack at his feet and drew it upon the rock beside him. He unbuckled the strap. "I've got a fresh can. Have I time enough for a pipe, Bruce?"

The question went unanswered, however, for as the pack unrolled, a hunting knife fell from its outer folds and clattered upon the hard surface of the rock, slipped farther, then slid down the inclined side of the rock into a small patch of azaleas growing at the base.

The sound drew the attention of all the hikers. Those who had not seen what had happened leaned forward for a better view; the others merely sat and looked from the azaleas to Turley. In the silence that followed, Turley slipped from his seat to the ground, reached among the flowers and fished out the knife, and held it up for all to see.

"I don't know," he said, his voice slightly shaken, "how that happened to be in my pack." He stared at it, his brows drawn into a scowl which darkened his usually placid face. "This is the knife, isn't it, Mr. Kramer, that you found back in Lost Valley?"

"Yeah, and the one that killed Hodges," asserted Jack Hammond, moving for a closer view. Plummer had sat forward electrified by the sight of the knife. Rogers was interested, not so much in the knife as in the hikers and their reactions. Turley offered the weapon to the chief ranger.

"As I say, Mr. Plummer," he remarked, "I don't know how it happened. I assure you I had no knowledge that it was there."

Plummer took the knife and turned it about, noting the initials scratched upon the handle, the long sharp blade which Leon Mullins had admitted cleansing of its blood. He glanced up at Turley, who still stood as if awaiting acceptance of his statement.

"Have you no idea at all how it got into your pack?"

"Not the slightest, sir. It wasn't there this morning."

"I can vouch for that, Mr. Plummer," said Douglas Kramer, pushing into the circle about the chief ranger. "We made up our packs at the same time. I remember Mr. Turley wondering if he should carry the fresh can of tobacco in his pocket or in the pack. That's what drew my attention to what he had in his pack. I saw everything, and there wasn't any knife."

"Somebody put it there, then," suggested Hammond, "when the pack was left lying around. And it wasn't me."

"Yeah?" said Al DeWitt unbelievingly.

"Believe it or not, it's so. We left our packs on the ground for a while at McGee Lake. Who went back to them? It wasn't me, was it?" He looked meaningly at Dudley, who sat apart from the others.

"If you mean me, Hammond, I'll consider the source of the information, which is highly irresponsible—"

"You mean you didn't do it?" asked Hammond.

"I didn't have the knife in my possession. I've not seen the knife since it disappeared at Merced Lake. Therefore, I couldn't have put it in anyone's pack. What's more, I wouldn't have done so if I could. I've no desire to incriminate any person. If I had found the knife, I would have brought it to the attention of Mr. Plummer without trying to implicate an innocent person."

The statement was slowly and carefully made, as if Dudley was at pains to include every possible angle.

The chief ranger recovered his own pack, opened it, and carefully placed the knife inside the roll, then drew the straps tight once more. He looked at Rogers.

"Have you any questions, Hunt?"

Rogers shook his head.

"Did anybody actually see this knife put in Mr. Turley's pack? Or does anybody have any knowledge of when and by whom it was done?"

The chief ranger's questions were greeted by a silence.

"Well, then," Plummer got to his feet, "if nobody knows anything perhaps we might as well move on. Meantime, if anybody recalls anything, save it and we will go into it at May Lake."

21

CLAUDIA BENSON was puzzled by the incident; why would anybody deliberately seek to implicate Mr. Turley? She fell in with him when the party moved on, and she detected underneath his usually calm manner that he was worried by the incident.

"It'll come out all right in the end," she sought to assure him.

"I hope so, Claudia. But I've begun to wonder if what's happened in Yosemite isn't destined to remain an unsolved mystery. Such things do happen, you know."

"Yes, unfortunately. But right before our eyes, almost, first Mr. Hodges, and then poor old Mr. Fulton are killed —and they haven't found out who did it."

"Do you know Mr. Hammond very well?"

"Very well? I detest him. He's one man I just can't stand."

"I don't seem able to get any sort of line on him. What he does. Where he comes from. He seems a little out of the class of people one would expect on a hike like this."

"Doesn't he!"

"I thought he deliberately tried to involve Mr. Dudley."

"I've noticed that Mr. Hammond seems to delight in tormenting people. I don't like him."

"I don't blame you, Claudia. I confess to a similar feeling."

They talked for a while as they hiked along the trail across a high ridge from which the great sweep of Yosemite lay stretched away below them. When Miss Forbes dropped back and joined them, Turley excused himself and hiked on ahead. Neither Miss Forbes nor Claudia spoke for a few minutes, then Claudia said:

"I don't know whether to call you Miss Forbes or Mrs. Mullins."

"Suit yourself; Forbes or Mullins, it makes no difference to me, Claudia." The reply was casual, but not curt or unfriendly. "In professional circles, as I explained at Glen Aulin, I'm Miss Forbes. I hate explaining. I do what I do, and let people think what they want to think. I'm not interested in their thoughts. There's this, though, to keep in mind; people remember you if you can get yourself talked about, or become the center of a controversy. That's a fundamental of publicity, and I've found publicity valuable in my work. Remember that, young lady, if you ever need publicity."

"I don't need it. I hope I never do."

"You know, I like you, and I'm going to tell you something."

"Yes?" said Claudia wonderingly.

"There's a certain young man in this party who would give his right arm for you."

"Douglas Kramer——"

"You guessed it the first time. I hope I haven't said too much."

"Perhaps not," said Claudia, feeling that her face was growing red, and wishing that Miss Forbes would take herself off and join somebody else. For the first day or two of the hike she had been attracted to the woman, but no longer, not since the night at Vogelsang when she had become so inquisitive.

"No more bad dreams, I suppose," said Miss Forbes, almost as though she were reading Claudia's thoughts.

"Not since Vogelsang. I'm too sound a sleeper now."

"I'd have sworn that somebody actually had been in your tent that night from the way you reacted. And then later you told me it was all a dream."

"Aren't you assuming a little too much?"

"Assuming? No, I'm just telling you my reactions to your strange behavior."

"Oh!" Claudia's anger began to smolder. "My behavior is my own," she said tartly. "And, like you, I'm not interested in other people's reactions."

Miss Forbes laughed. "Right on the chin, wasn't it? But I don't mind. It's things like that that make me believe I could be fond of you. But there's just one thing I want to ask you: What was it Uncle Tom gave you that morning after we had got away from Vogelsang? You see, I didn't let Uncle Tom very far out of sight. I was sitting near you, but you didn't know it. I think I have a right to an answer."

"All right, here's your answer: Things that I consider to be strictly my own business I don't share with other people."

"I think you're foolish," protested Miss Forbes. Soon thereafter Miss Forbes became interested in a clump of shooting stars beside the trail and Claudia walked on ahead.

Claudia hiked on alone. She wondered as her boots clumped indignantly on the rocky soil what Miss Forbes knew about the monkey carved from a piece of jade. She recalled distinctly that old Mr. Fulton had chosen a time when they seemed quite alone. But Miss Forbes had been spying. That was despicable. On an impulse she pulled the jade monkey out of her pocket and held it in her hand. The sun shone upon its dark green, silky beauty. The thing was exquisitely carved; the tiniest of lines made the monkey's face that of an odd little old man, wistful and pensive and patient.

She put the keepsake back into her pocket again. Once before the thought had crossed her mind that the monkey might have had something to do with the murders, but she had discarded it as farfetched. She now examined the idea once more and again she reasoned that while it might conceivably have had something to do with the death of old Mr. Fulton, it could have had no connection whatever with the death of Mr. Hodges. The belief among the hikers was that the same person had killed both men. Mr. Hodges hadn't had the monkey. She had had it in her pocket. Besides, old Mr. Fulton hadn't said anything about Mr. Hodges when he gave it to her.

Miss Forbes just now, though, had presented her with a new idea about the monkey. Perhaps it was a cherished family heirloom with which she had been familiar, and she had suspected, or perhaps Mr. Fulton had actually told her, where it was to be found in case of his death. It was all rather vague; she realized that she didn't have any analytic powers in such matters. It occurred to her, though, that she ought to ask somebody about it, now that Mr. Fulton was dead. Doug Kramer would know more than anybody else about it, that is, the legal angles involved. If it was a valued heirloom, did it belong to the old man's estate? Or had his giving it to her as he did on the trail that morning been a gift which could not be set aside? She thought she'd like to keep it as something by which to remember a kindly old man, a fellow hiker. She guessed she'd better consult Doug, though, to make sure, since he had drawn the will and probably would have something to do with administering the estate.

As she walked along puzzling over the problem she overtook Leon Mullins. Hitherto he had seemed such a quiet, shy sort of man that she hadn't really got acquainted with him. There hadn't been any humor in him; about camp he was always sober and slow-spoken.

"Have you seen my wife in the last half hour?" he asked, joining Claudia and walking beside her, for the trail was wide.

"I left her behind just a little while ago."

"She's all right, then." He seemed satisfied, and they walked on silently together for several minutes. "You're not afraid to walk with me, are you?"

"No, why?" Claudia was startled by the question.

"I'm the murderer."

Claudia twisted her head suddenly to look at the serious face of the man at her side. The rugged features were completely calm; there was no hint of humor in his light blue eyes.

"Are you serious?" Claudia's heart began to pound.

"Yes."

A strange chill ran the length of Claudia's spine. A sudden impulse seized upon her and she wanted to run, but she did not dare do so. To yield to panic might be fatal. He might strike her in the back, or seize her by the throat and strangle her. The powerful hands hung at the end of his long arms, and swung, as she fancied, with a sinister motion.

"You're joking!" she managed to say. Her voice sounded queer.

"Oh, no. The chief ranger is sure of it, so it must be so."

Claudia suddenly felt like beating the man; only the fact that she never had done anything so violent in her whole life prevented her now from belaboring him with her hands, or kicking him.

"You frightened me!"

"But maybe the man's right." The voice was persuasive.

"Mr. Mullins, I don't enjoy this sort of humor. It's not funny. It's unpleasant, to say the least, and if you'll excuse me, your wife is somewhere behind us. I'm going on."

Claudia quickened her pace, and drew rapidly away from the middle-aged cowboy. Afterward in the confusion of piecing together her thoughts she wondered if she had heard him laughing at her. She thrust her hands deeper into her pockets, and her left one closed about the jade monkey. The sound was that of laughter, and yet it wasn't laughter. It was eerie, and a cold chill seemed to settle on her skin underneath the pack on her shoulders.

Sometime afterward Claudia realized that she was being carried. Everything was dark. The air was cold and so thin that it scarcely filled her lungs and she had to breathe hard to satisfy their hunger. Maybe somebody said it was the altitude, or she might have thought of it by herself. She wasn't sure. It was like trying to remember a dream fast fading from her waking consciousness. Then there was the nightmare, or did that come first? Time was uncertain. Jack Hammond said: "You're all right, babe; quit kicking." He'd kissed her as he carried her in his arms. She'd never be able to wipe away the kiss. That was his kind, to take advantage of her. A wave of furious but helpless resentment surged over her.

Next she was being carried on a litter. It was hard,

something was pressing into her back, and her head ached. She struggled to get up, to escape from Jack Hammond. He might try again to kiss her. A hand on her shoulder pushed her down, and somebody said something to somebody about lying still. Anyhow, the voice said, it wasn't far to camp. And everybody was glad. She could feel their gladness. A blackness blacker than a starless night hovered at her elbow, then moved crabwise like a curtain of fog and shut out everything. Once a mountain seemed to fill all the horizon before her blurred vision, and then it momentarily became Beryl Lindsay, who tucked something about her neck. After that she was carried swinging and swaying in the litter, and she was so relaxed that she never wanted to move a muscle again as long as she lived. It was the way she had wanted to be sometimes when she came home tired from the office; it felt almost as though she would break down, all of her, the skin and the muscles that held her in the shape of a woman, and she would just spread out like butter melting in the sun. It was a heavenly feeling just to melt and run like that in utter relaxation. "The blanket's too hot; she's sweating," said Al DeWitt.

Things were cool and dark next. She wasn't being carried. That horrible something no longer pressed into her back; there wasn't any jolting; her head ached comfortably without throbs and starts. It was growing dark outside the tent. A great regret filled her. It was sunset time and May Lake was where they could see the sunset once more—that unbelievable sunset of the High Sierras, all deep blue, deeper and bluer than any sea, and rose that made you catch your breath. She wanted to see it. Maybe she'd never see another one. She had to see this last sunset. That was why she had come on the hike.

"Now, then, just lie back quietly, Miss Benson."

It was a strange voice and Claudia opened her eyes and stared at the man. He was dressed in the gray-green uniform of the park service. He was older than Bruce Milbank, older even than Mr. Plummer, but he had a sweet smile, and a kindly face; there was something wholesome and tremendously vigorous about him that made her want to live and hike and run and play again.

"Are you the doctor?"

"Why, no. I'm Superintendent Haverly. I've sent for a doctor. He'll be here just as soon as he can get up from the Valley floor"

"I'm all right. Really I am. It's silly for me to stay in bed. I want to see the sunset."

"Maybe you'd better not talk."

"Why not?"

"How do you feel?"

"Fine. Except that my head aches a little."

Claudia heard others in the tent. She saw Miss Lindsay, and over her shoulder she could see Professor Rogers.

"Maybe you'd better not talk, Claudia," advised Beryl Lindsay solemnly. "You've had a hard knock on your head."

Claudia put her hand up to her head experimentally. She felt a swelling in the edge of her hair above her forehead.

"Is that what happened to me?"

"Don't you know what happened?" asked the superintendent.

"Everything's so mixed up." Claudia felt very confused. Her hands were underneath the blanket. Once more she tried to dig deeper into the comfort of the bed. She thrust her hands into her pockets and was surprised to find that she was still fully dressed.

Rogers came and stood over her and smiled; he said something to the superintendent which Claudia didn't hear, and the superintendent, looking up from his chair, agreed with him.

Claudia's fingers clenched and unclenched in her pockets. It was good to feel them move and to feel the strength in them. She was growing stronger all over; no longer was she melting and spreading out like butter in the sun. Suddenly she thrust deeper into her left pocket and felt around. And then in the right. A frown creased her brow. Beryl Lindsay leaned over and said:

"What is it, dear?"

"I've lost the green monkey."

22

THE chief ranger had a feeling that things were at a climax; his reaction to the events of the last few hours was reinforced by signs of suppressed excitement in Huntoon Rogers. Outwardly Rogers appeared unmoved, but there was a look in his mild blue eyes that betrayed what went on beneath his calm exterior.

Superintendent Haverly had put an authoritative foot down upon any questioning of Claudia Benson before the doctor arrived, and he was right. Head injuries were ticklish business, and there was a sizable bump on the girl's head. So it was not until after dinner that they had an opportunity to question her. Until then, though, they had been able only to speculate upon what had happened earlier that afternoon on the trail.

"She'll be all right," Doctor Jorgenson said. "In fact, she's all right now."

"We want to question her."

"Go ahead."

There were only four of them in the tent with Claudia, who still lay under the blanket. Superintendent Haverly sat back and listened. Rogers did most of the talking.

"What happened, Claudia?" he asked quietly.

"I don't know."

The chief ranger felt let down by this beginning. He had hoped she might be able to solve their problem in a few words.

"Who hit you on the head?" he asked.

"Did somebody hit me on the head, Mr. Plummer?"

Rogers took up the questioning. "Tell us, Claudia, what's the last thing you remember happening on the trail when you were navigating under your own power, so to speak."

The girl looked at him speculatively. She was trying to remember.

"Well, I have a clear memory of talking with Miss Forbes. When she dropped back, Mr. Turley went on ahead. She and I talked and then I walked away from her and caught up with Mr. Mullins. We hiked together. But when he tried to scare me by saying that he was the murderer, I got mad——"

"Did he say that?" asked Superintendent Haverly quickly.

"When I started to get mad he said that, according to Mr. Plummer, he was the murderer."

"Go on. Sorry to interrupt."

"I walked away from him, although I wanted to beat him for trying to frighten me. Then I thought I heard him laugh behind me. It was the creepiest sort of sound. It scared me, really. And then I was being carried by someone. I thought it was Jack Hammond. And he—he kissed me——"

"Oh, no!" objected the chief ranger.

"Maybe I dreamed it. It was sort of nightmarish. And that's all."

"You don't have any recollection of anybody leaping out at you from behind a tree, or a rock, and striking you?"

"No, Professor Rogers, I haven't. There was just that laugh—and then I was being carried."

That was the exasperating thing about what had happened to the girl. She couldn't remember what was important. The chief ranger could understand, though, why it was. He'd got knocked cold himself once by an automobile in Sacramento, and all he'd ever been able to recall of the accident was a brief glimpse of the approaching car when it was still about fifty feet away. What occurred in the intervening seconds, as well as the moment of violent impact itself, were completely gone from his consciousness. He always had supposed that the final few seconds were filled with terror at the thought of sudden death, and that some merciful mechanism of the mind had deleted it from consciousness more completely than a censor's pencil could erase forbidden information in war time.

It was quite possible that some such thing had happened to the girl. If so she never would be able to tell them about it. Perhaps the sudden appearance of her attacker beside the trail; or an unexpected hand that reached out and seized her; or the fleeting vision of the arm descending might at one time have been in the girl's consciousness, but it was gone. Rogers probed skilfully about the circumstances, going back patiently over each step, endeavoring to aid her to recapture the scene, but it was hopeless.

"And now, what about the jade monkey?" Rogers asked at last.

"It's gone."

Far from being distressed over the fact, Rogers seemed to acquire a new thirst for information.

"How did you happen to have it?"

"Mr. Fulton gave it to me."

"When? How? Just tell me about it."

"The first time, I found it in my pack at Merced Lake, but I didn't know where it had come from. He'd slipped it in there when I wasn't looking," Claudia went on after a moment. "But it was stolen from me, you see, at Vogelsang."

"Stolen?"

"Yes, I— Somebody was in my tent. I waked up, and he threatened to kill me if I screamed. He just whispered to me, so I couldn't tell who it was. And when he was gone I ran over to Miss Forbes' tent and told her. She was so inquisitive that I got scared and when morning came I told her I had dreamed it all." She halted and looked oddly at Rogers. "I'm sorry, Professor, that I deceived you too. I told you it was all a dream. But that was because I had promised Mr. Fulton not to say anything about the jade monkey to anybody, and I couldn't admit that somebody was in my tent without telling what really it was all about."

The girl talked in a rush as though eager to get into words something that had long been troubling her. Rogers remained quiet, then he gently prodded her into another recollection.

"I think Mr. Fulton knew who it was," she went on. "Because the man came back into the men's dormitory, and dropped it—the monkey—on the floor—and tried to find it, and couldn't, because it had fallen into Mr. Fulton's shoe. He discovered it next morning, Mr. Fulton, I mean. And after that had happened he gave it back to me. He didn't want me to talk about it to anybody—that he'd given it to me, or that I even had it. He wouldn't tell me why, and I never knew. Only this afternoon I was thinking of asking Doug Kramer what I ought to do about it, now that Mr. Fulton is dead, but I didn't have a chance to."

"When did you last have the monkey in your possession?"

"Right after I left Mr. Mullins on the trail. I took it out of my pocket and looked at it, then put it back again."

"Are you positive?"

"Yes."

"Was that just before your accident?"

"Yes."

"Do you remember just how you were walking, the very last thing before the accident must have occurred?" Rogers was back again, the chief ranger realized, probing for the vital facts that had vanished from the girl's mind.

"I was walking along the trail. I had my hands in my pockets. I remember I still held the monkey in my left hand inside my pocket."

"Could anybody have seen you looking at the monkey?"

"I don't think so. Mr. Mullins couldn't. He was too far behind."

"And you didn't hear any footsteps behind you? Or anybody moving near by just off the trail?"

"No, not a thing that I can remember."

"Did Mr. Fulton indicate in any way who the person might have been who stole the jade monkey at Vogelsang?"

"No."

"Did he indicate that he was afraid of this person?"

"No. That is, not actually afraid. But he was awfully puzzled about the monkey and the man who had given it to him. He said something about a telephone call—as if it was a threat. And a note under his door at the hotel, which he destroyed. He was doing things by hunches. It

was just a hunch that he gave the monkey to me and a
hunch that made him bring it along. I thought he was like
a person just waking up to the fact that something terrible
had been put over on him."

To the chief ranger it seemed that they were at the end
of their line of questioning. Miss Benson had told all she
knew. She was growing restless. Superintendent Haverly
spoke.

"If this thief who dropped the jade monkey in the dormitory at Vogelsang after he'd been to so much trouble
to steal it from Miss Benson really wanted the thing,
would he have given up the search so easily? Wouldn't he
have looked around for it later in daylight, say?"

"It's quite likely that he would," Rogers agreed.

"Well, did he?"

"Perhaps we can develop the fact later this evening."

"He might have started away with the party and then
gone back for a look," the superintendent persisted. "Why
can't we call up Vogelsang tonight, Floyd, and ask if anybody remembers any of the party coming back to camp
after the crowd got started?"

"We could—"

"Oh," said Claudia, remembering something. "Mr.
Stoner."

"What about Stoner?" Plummer asked.

"He started back to go around by the Lyell Fork because the fishing was better that way."

"He'd have to go back to Vogelsang to do that," said
Plummer.

"But I don't think he really did. He went back, and then
later on he caught up with us on the Rafferty Creek trail."

"Stoner," said Plummer. "I'll call up Vogelsang."

"And I'm not going to miss everything at this camp," said Claudia emphatically.

"What aren't you going to miss?" Superintendent Haverly asked banteringly.

"I want to see the fire fall from here tonight."

"You probably can. It's a clear evening, and from the promontory behind the camp here you can see all the way down Tenaya Canyon into the Valley, and watch the fire fall. I'll go with you myself, if I can persuade you to take me along."

"I'd love to have you."

"It's a date. Meantime you'd better rest. I'll see if the manager's wife can come and sit with you while the rest of us do a bit of talking around the fire outside."

"But I'm coming out to the campfire."

"If the doctor says so."

Plummer went off to telephone, leaving the superintendent to settle the matter. He rang the camp at Vogelsang and finally had the manager on the wire. He put his questions, careful that his voice did not carry to the hikers outside assembling about the burning logs.

"Yes, there was a fellow who came back," was the answer.

"After the party had left?"

"Yes. About half an hour or so."

"Who was he?"

"I don't remember the name. Sort of a skinny fellow with a fishing pole and tackle."

"What did he do there?"

"He was going to go down the Lyell Fork, but when he

found out it would be five miles farther he decided not to go. Said he guessed he'd take the Rafferty Creek trail after all."

"Did he go back into the dormitory tent before he left?"

"I don't know. He started off, and we didn't see him after that. We were all of us up in the dining room when he showed up."

So Stoner would have some explaining to do, thought Plummer, as he went outside. He noted that Claudia Benson had won her point, for she sat between Doctor Jorgenson and Superintendent Haverly, looking at the campfire and showing little sign of her narrow escape from death.

A silence greeted the chief ranger as he approached the fire, and he realized what was expected of him once more.

"It's rather a grim commentary on this hike," he said after a moment, "that we should have to have these nightly quizzes into the misfortunes that have dogged the party ever since it set out from Happy Isles. There's no need wasting time in preliminaries. You all know what happened this afternoon. That Miss Benson is sitting with us tonight at the campfire, little worse for her experience, was not the intention, I'm sure, of the person who sooner or later will have so much to answer for.

"But—Mr. Hammond, you found Miss Benson, I believe."

"Yes, I did."

"Tell us about it."

"Well, I was coming along by myself in that stretch. We'd got sort of spread out, all of us, if you remember, after we stopped for lunch—and there she was."

"She was lying in the trail?"

"I didn't say that. I just all of a sudden saw her. I saw

ne foot sticking out from behind a rock. I recognized her
hoe and I said: 'Hey, babe, what's going on?' The foot
lidn't move, so I stopped to see, and there she was out
old."

"Describe the scene, please."

"Well, there was rocks and trees, of course. Anybody
ould have hid there and jumped out and conked her as she
vent by. The first thing I noticed was the pockets in her
ants pulled out like they'd been searched. Then I noticed
er pack was open and the stuff all scattered. It scared me
t first. I thought I might be accused of doing the job. But,
ell, why should that worry me? I knew she might need a
loctor, so I picked her up and started carrying her. There
vasn't anybody in sight when I stepped out on the trail, but
ust around a bend in the trail I ran into Stoner. I put her
lown, and soon some of the others showed up. Leon Mul-
ins and Miss Forbes, and Turley and Dudley, and I don't
emember who all. I think you and Rogers showed up, and
ou know the story from there, the same as I do."

"It's your opinion, then, Mr. Hammond, that the mo-
ive was robbery?"

"It looked that way to me. I think he tried to kill her
oo."

"Probably," replied the chief ranger grimly.

23

"Mr. Stoner," the chief ranger turned to the small figure that sat like a statue staring into the fire.

Stoner came suddenly to life. "Yes, sir?"

"What can you tell us about Miss Benson's accident?"

"Not a thing. Sorry. I didn't hear anything, or see anything. I didn't know anything had happened until Jack showed up carrying her."

"How long had you been sitting there by the trail?"

"Ten minutes. Maybe fifteen."

"Did anybody pass you in that time?"

"No, sir."

"How far was it from where you were sitting to where Miss Benson was found?"

"Sixty yards, I guess. I went back to where Jack had found her and sort of estimated the distance while I was looking around. I picked up her things."

"While you were sitting beside the trail did you hear any suspicious sounds as the attacker lay in wait?"

"No, sir."

"What were you doing there?"

"Just sitting, resting. I sort of flirted with the wild life. There was a gray squirrel, and a jay. I had 'em puzzled by laughing at them the way a mynah bird laughs. Indian mynahs are good talkers. Ever hear one laugh?" Without waiting for a reply Stoner uttered an eerie sound that resembled human laughter but was so softened and modified that it sounded as if it came from another world.

The chief ranger's gaze had strayed to Claudia Benson. The girl suddenly shrank in alarm, and put her hands over her face. There was an odd silence following Stoner's exhibition of mimicry. Plummer spoke to Claudia.

"Is that the sound you heard, Miss Benson?"

"Yes."

"I see." The chief ranger turned back to Stoner. "Were you alone all the while this was happening, Mr. Stoner?"

"Yes, sir."

"Mr. Mullins——"

The cowboy started, and glanced at Plummer standing across the fire from him. It was as if he had come back to his surroundings from a long day dream.

"Yes, sir. What have I done now?"

"What happened this afternoon after Miss Benson and you parted on the trail?"

"Nothing. She didn't like my pretending that I was the murderer and walked on ahead. Almost ran, in fact, to get away from me. I didn't know I had that effect on young folks. I'm sorry now that I scared her."

"But what happened?"

"Nothing. I sat down and waited until Mrs. Mullins came along. She sat down with me for a few minutes, then we went on. Farther on we came across the crowd that was gathering about Miss Benson. Hammond had laid her down, and they were planning to fix up a litter."

"Yes, I know. But in that time you sat with your wife, did anybody pass you on the trail?"

"No, sir."

"How far from where you and your wife sat was it to where Miss Benson was struck down?"

"Oh——" the cowboy tilted his head back and gazed off

into the darkness.

"It couldn't have been far, Leon," interposed Miss Forbes. "Not more than a short city block."

"About that," agreed Mullins. "Say a hundred yards."

"Mr. Dudley," the chief ranger turned to the next in the circle about the fire. "Where were you at the time?"

"I was farther back on the trail. Walked up to the accident behind the Mullinses with Turley. He'd caught up with me a short distance back."

"Mr. DeWitt, how about you and Mrs. DeWitt?"

"It all happened behind us. We didn't know anything had happened until we saw the crowd coming in with Miss Benson. That's one time, ranger, you can't hang anything on me."

"I congratulate you," said Plummer soberly.

"Mr. Kramer?"

"Sorry, sir. But I had gone by before it all happened." He looked hopefully at Claudia, but she was staring at the fire.

"Miss Lindsay, what can you tell us?"

The school teacher had sat silently in the circle, following with her eyes as the chief ranger turned from one to another of the party. She stirred, and glanced at the park naturalist.

"Bruce and I were sitting on a rock. It must have been just beyond Mr. Stoner, because it was only a short distance back to where Mr. Hammond put Claudia down on the trail. I was waiting for her to come along, because I hadn't had a visit with her for several hours. I decided to go back and meet her, and Bruce started back with me."

"Did you hear Mr. Stoner imitating a mynah bird?"

"No, I didn't."

"Was Mr. Stoner sitting beside the trail when you saw him?"

"No, he was standing. Sort of looking down the trail as if he was expecting someone, and Mr. Hammond walked up carrying Claudia. What I want to know, though, Mr. Plummer, is where was Jack Hammond?"

"How do you mean, Miss Lindsay?"

"Well, Claudia left Mr. Mullins and ran on ahead, and Mr. Mullins sat down to wait for his wife. Nobody passed him. And if nobody passed Mr. Stoner, who was the nearest person on the other side of the place where the accident occurred, then where was Mr. Hammond?"

"Yeah, where were you, Jack?" teased DeWitt.

"I was right where I said I was, coming along the trail when I saw her foot sticking out from behind a rock. I called out—"

"Yes, I know, Mr. Hammond," interrupted Plummer, "but where were you? Were you behind the Mullinses?"

"I don't think so. I didn't pass 'em anywhere. Hadn't seen either of 'em since lunch."

"But you must have been somewhere. Where were you? Did you see Miss Benson go by?"

"That was the way of it. I was sitting behind a tree when she went by. I wondered what was her hurry. I got up and followed, because I wanted to talk to her. She'd been thumbing her nose at me ever since we got started, and no dame can do that in an outfit like this where we're all supposed to be pals."

"And you—"

"No, I didn't do it. I don't know who did, either."

"How long after Miss Benson went by until you followed?"

"Three or four minutes."

"She was practically running, I understand. Did you run too?"

"I walked. Whoever conked her must have just done the job, see, and searched her when he heard me coming. He couldn't have been gone a minute—"

"Did you try to follow and find out who it was?"

"No, I didn't. The girl was more important; I wanted to save her life. She was still breathing."

"And you didn't hear anything, or see anything suspicious off the trail, as if somebody was running away?"

"No."

"Mr. Stoner, another question." Plummer turned back to the fisherman abruptly. "About Vogelsang."

"Yes?"

"After the party left camp that morning, you went back, intending to take the trail down the Lyell Fork."

"Yeah, but I didn't. They told me at Vogelsang it was five miles farther by that trail, and so I didn't go. I tagged along down Rafferty Creek."

"And at Vogelsang when you returned, you stopped in at the dormitory tent where you'd spent the night. Tell me what for."

"Well," the man seemed surprised at the turn the questioning had taken, "it was like this. I'd mislaid one of my flies, a black gnat, somewhere, and I thought maybe I'd left it in the tent."

"Was that the only reason?"

"What other reason would I have?"

"Forget it, Stoner. Did you find the black gnat?"

"Yes, sir."

The chief ranger paused and looked at Rogers inquiringly. "Any questions, Hunt?"

"None, Floyd."

"Mr. Haverly?"

"I think not." The superintendent looked at his watch. "I promised to show Miss Benson the fire fall from May Lake."

There was a stir about the campfire as the hikers realized that the night's investigation had ended, and the entire party joined the superintendent and Claudia and made their way to the promontory behind the camp where they waited in the darkness, gazing off down the sweep of Tenaya Canyon to where a star-filled sky ended at the sheer rock walls of Glacier Point. There a tiny pinpoint of light flickered as the distant fire burned down to embers.

Only the murmur of occasional voices broke the stillness; now and then a flashlight was snapped on and a watch consulted. It was still several minutes, somebody said. The chief ranger found himself with Rogers at the extreme edge of the group.

"It looks to me that you're right, Hunt," he said. "About the green monkey. The fellow tried to kill the girl to get it."

"I'm sure of it."

"Then it follows that whoever's got it now is the fellow we want."

"Probably."

"It's a bit unusual to order a search of everybody," he said softly, as if thinking aloud. "It would have to be accomplished suddenly. Before the thing could be done away with." The chief ranger's voice was scarcely above a whisper. He would have said more but just at the moment someone raised a cry:

"There it is, the fire fall!"

Far off in the blackness the tiny point of light seemed to glow brighter and then lengthened downward in a line from the burned-out fire on Glacier Point. It lengthened slowly. The hikers watched in silence.

"But it's so short!" exclaimed Beryl Lindsay.

"Yet it's a thousand feet," said Bruce Milbank. "It's the distance—about ten miles."

"But such a tiny little line of fire there in the dark. I can still see it."

"So can I," said Claudia.

"It's going, though," said Beryl Lindsay after a few moments.

"And it's gone," pronounced Superintendent Haverly.

"Thank you for bringing me up here," said Claudia to the superintendent. "It makes up for what happened to me today. But I don't want to go back to the Valley floor tomorrow. I don't want the party to break up, even though we've had so much bad luck."

"Why don't we sing some songs?" suggested Dudley. "I'm not going to bed tonight if somebody will sit up with me."

"I'll sit up with you," said Beryl Lindsay. She snapped on her flashlight. "Bill Turley, how about you?"

"Sure. Count me in. Why don't we go down to the campfire, though? It's chilly up here."

There was a movement among the dark forms. Suddenly Beryl Lindsay's voice rose above the others.

"No, I want to see what you've got. I saw something in your hand."

"It wasn't anything," protested Hammond.

"But it was. I want to see it. You had it in your hand.

Was it a piece of jade?"

There was the sound of a scuffle, and flashlights were turned upon the pair. "I've got it!" The school teacher's voice was exultant as she wrested something from Hammond's hand.

"Why, it's a little monkey carved from jade," she said, looking at it in the rays of her flashlight. "It's lovely. Where did you get it?"

"It's mine," said Claudia.

"Yeah?" Hammond countered.

"How did you get it?" Claudia demanded heatedly. "I found it."

"Yes, you did," said Al DeWitt sarcastically.

The jade monkey lay in Beryl Lindsay's broad plump hand, illumined by the flashlights that had been trained upon it as the hikers crowded about her to see what it was.

"It's mine," repeated Claudia. "Mr. Fulton gave it to me just the day before he died."

Rogers moved into the circle, stood for a moment looking at the bit of jade over the school teacher's shoulder, then reached into the open palm and picked it up.

"If you don't mind, Claudia, I'll take charge of it." He held it in the rays of the flashlights and gazed at its silky smooth green texture. "You'll get it back. You wouldn't want to lose it again."

"I found it, I tell you," persisted Hammond. "Just as I was going to pick Claudia up. It was under her. She was lying on it. I was going to give it back to her."

"I don't believe it," said DeWitt.

Rogers' voice cut through the argument. "On second thought," he said, "I think Superintendent Haverly had better take charge of it. Is it all right with you, Claudia?"

"Yes, Professor."

"What's so important about a jade monkey?" asked Mrs. DeWitt.

"It's not important; it's just a little keepsake," said Claudia, intuitively settling the argument to the satisfaction of the other hikers. "And I'm going down to the campfire, and sing songs with Mr. Dudley. And with Doug." She reached out and seized Kramer's arm. "You don't want the hike to end, either, do you, Doug?"

The crowd moved below to the campfire. Rogers and the chief ranger and Superintendent Haverly remained behind on the promontory. A song had been started on the way down below, and the voices came back as the trio stood in the darkness. Rogers spoke.

"And now, Mr. Haverly, unless you want to get your throat cut tonight, you'll have to get out of camp."

"Is it as bad as that?"

"I imagine the killer's desperate. Can you get down to the Valley floor tonight?"

"Yes. It's only a mile out to the Tioga Road. Bert Cole drove me up this afternoon and then went on to Tuolumne Meadows. I'll phone him to come back and pick me up. Jorgenson probably will want to go too."

"We'll go with you down to the road," said Plummer, "and make sure Bert picks you up."

"That's the best solution, Mr. Haverly," said Rogers soberly. "I regret that I'm obliged to suggest to the superintendent of Yosemite National Park what he must do. But the jade monkey must not stay overnight in this camp; and it must be kept safely until we've all got down to the Valley floor and seen what we shall see."

"What's so important about it?"

"I'm not a gambler, Mr. Haverly, but tonight I feel that I'm risking everything on the turn of a card, as it were. If the jade monkey doesn't provide a solution of what's happened in Yosemite, then I don't know where there is a solution. We'd have to start all over again."

"Couldn't you find out that fact here—now?"

"No. It's only a hunch—a strong hunch. But that's the way it has to be. I mean the solution has to be in that piece of jade."

The superintendent was silent. Rogers went on. "By the way, when the party gets down on the Valley floor tomorrow afternoon, could you arrange a magic lantern show for the hikers?"

"A magic lantern show?"

"I mean one of those illustrated talks the rangers give."

"Of course. What will it be about?"

"I'll do the talking, if you don't mind. I'd like as many slides of scenes along this hike, the camps, and the trails, say, as the boys at the Museum can dig up from their collection."

"I'll arrange it myself. But if this jade monkey can reveal the murderer, and he knows I'm carrying it away tonight, won't that tip him off?"

"Yes, but he doesn't dare leave. He's trapped and he knows it. Before you leave May Lake tonight will you invite the party to an illustrated talk tomorrow afternoon? At your office, say. Make it a polite but official must, so that we'll have a full attendance."

24

BRUCE MILBANK wondered a bit as he sat in the circle around the campfire; he not only wondered why the superintendent was in such a hurry to get down to the Valley floor, but he wondered why the illustrated talk at the end of the hike. That had never been done before. He wondered if it had any relation to the death of Hodges and of old man Fulton. It hadn't been lost on him that the superintendent had remained behind on the promontory with Rogers and the chief ranger. And he wondered, if all this was so, whether there would be any reaction upon the part of the killer, who must be sitting in the circle about the campfire? Would he betray himself by his attitude? Would he show that he was worried, or perhaps frightened?

Rogers and Plummer had gone down the trail with the superintendent and Dr. Jorgenson. Plummer said that he and Rogers would be back. Meanwhile Milbank's gaze went slowly about the circle. Turley had borrowed a mandolin from the camp cook and was leading the singing. When the hikers couldn't agree on what they wanted to sing, Turley filled in with a ballad from his inexhaustible repertory. Frederick Dudley, the most reserved of all the hikers at the beginning, was now the most enthusiastic of the singers, the gayest, in fact. Even Leon Mullins and his wife, Miss Forbes, sang lustily, and Jack Hammond surprised everybody with an unsuspected talent as a choirmaster.

Milbank's eyes came back to Claudia Benson. She was

singing with the others, she and Doug Kramer, beating time occasionally with her right hand. The thing that gave Milbank something of a start, however, was that she sat so close to Kramer. He rubbed his eyes. Did he see aright? She was snuggled against him. Kramer's arm was around the girl and her left hand was folded over his close to her side. This was one minor headache that had cleared up. He wasn't supposed to be a matchmaker, but he couldn't help recalling that morning at Happy Isles when Claudia Benson indignantly proposed to quit the party before it even got started, just because Kramer had showed up as a member.

It was the old hike stuff proving out once more; you couldn't herd a crowd of people together for a week on mountain trails where they broke with the routine of everyday life without smoothing out a lot of kinks. There was something in mountain air and far visions and hard hiking in high country that recreated human beings. The mob that yearly swarmed into the Valley, ate ice cream cones, drank pop, rode over to Mirror Lake, looked at Bridalveil through automobile windows and sat around waiting for the cafeterias to open might as well stay home for all the good Yosemite could do for them.

Bruce Milbank went to bed thinking about these things rather than murder and sudden death. It had been terrifying when it struck, and unsettling, but in the end healthy human factors were reasserting themselves among the hikers. He thought that when it was all over and the hikers in the months to come recalled the days of their hike, it would not be of murder that they would think, but instead of humming birds at ten thousand feet, of sunsets and still nights, of wild azaleas, of roaring cascades of white water, of hunger and ham and eggs for breakfast, and the smell of pine forests in crisp cold air.

Plummer and Rogers had come back before Milbank turned in. Some of the crowd had got sleepy and gone to bed, but when Milbank last saw the group around the fire he recognized Turley, Dudley, Miss Lindsay, and Huntoon Rogers; they were singing "Sweet Adeline" in barbershop, with Rogers leading in a sort of roaring baritone. The last that Milbank remembered was the opening lines of "Drink to Me Only with Thine Eyes," and then he awakened to the new day and the stillness of early morning.

The park naturalist had no regrets that this was the last day of the hike; for him it was only a duty ending. Under other circumstances he would have felt somewhat the reluctance that the hikers felt. At breakfast the prospect of parting before the day was done was openly deplored by Beryl Lindsay. Her eyes were heavy-lidded and when Claudia Benson asked her if she hadn't slept well the school teacher brightened up and boasted of the quartet of which she had been a member.

"Just imagine! We didn't get to bed until two o'clock. I want to put down in my diary all the songs we sang. Bill Turley, you're a marvel." She beamed at the bronzed figure at the end of the table. "And, Professor Rogers, you and Mr. Dudley can belong to my quartet any time. We would make good on the radio."

"Oh, I'm sure of it," Rogers grinned. "As the High Sierra Yodelers—or something."

Chief Ranger Plummer called Milbank to one side when breakfast was over. "Here's what you're to do, Bruce," he said quietly. "Get the party down to the Valley floor as early as you can this afternoon without hurrying them too much. After all, it's their hike and they're entitled to all that's coming. Keep them together as a group and bring them over to Mr. Haverly's office at government center. Rogers and I are pulling out right away. We'll be down before lunch. Try to make it by three-thirty. We'll be expecting you. Remind the hikers of Mr. Haverly's invitation last night."

"It has to do with what happened at Merced Lake and Glen Aulin?"

"Yes."

"Do I keep an eye out for anybody in particular?"

"No."

Down the trail onto the floor of Yosemite Valley, past Mirror Lake, glass-like under the towering block that is Half Dome, Bruce Milbank led his hikers. They had become quiet toward the last, and walked doggedly in a compact group as if they sensed what lay ahead. Cars drove along the roads, bicyclists idled upon the paths; scenes like these always seemed strange to Milbank on first getting down from a week in the back country. Past the post office and the Museum and to the Administration building almost within the spray from Yosemite Falls, leaping in a white ribbon from the rim of the rock wall, the party made its way. They entered the wide door, crossed the small lobby, and went down the hallway to the superintendent's office at the far end.

"Come in," said Superintendent Haverly, opening his door and standing aside. "Welcome."

Milbank brought up the rear. He noted that the big flat-top desk had been pushed back and chairs arranged in a semi-circle to face a small screen at the opposite side of the room. The machine for the slides of an illustrated lecture was in place behind the chairs, and Rogers and Plummer were standing to the rear of it. Milbank joined them.

"Thanks, Bruce," said Plummer approvingly. "Right on schedule. They're all here, are they?"

"Yes, sir."

The superintendent closed the door, advanced a few steps, and stood before the small audience.

"I want to say only a few words. I invited you to come here. Hiking parties don't usually come like this at the end of their hike, but after what has happened in the course of your vacation you're entitled to an explanation. To those of you who have been inconvenienced, and shocked, and perhaps frightened by the death of Mr. Hodges at Merced Lake and of Mr. Fulton at Glen Aulin, I can only say that I am sorry. At the same time I want to congratulate you on your courage in the face of those unnerving events and thank you for your patience and forbearance while a most difficult problem was in the process of solution. Professor Rogers will take over. Before he is through you will know what went wrong with your hike and who is to blame for it."

Milbank helped adjust the blinds at the windows, and at the chief ranger's request moved in behind the machine to manipulate the slides.

"They're all in order the way you want them, are they, Professor?"

"Yes, Bruce. Don't change slides until I tell you." Rogers cleared his throat softly, gazed over the heads of his audience in the semi-darkened room and then began to speak.

"I hope you don't mind my talking from behind you,"

he said. "There is no intention upon my part of pouncing on any of you suddenly and proclaiming you the guilty person. So, be comfortable, please, and if you don't mind, I'll begin at the very beginning. The beginning is before Pearl Harbor.

"In Contra Costa County there was a man we'll call Hugh Buckingham, although it is doubtful that that was his real name, who in that pre-war period raised squabs for the San Francisco market. He supplied the trans-Pacific liners too. As a matter of fact, the last Japanese boat to leave San Francisco carried away a crate of Mr. Buckingham's squabs. The fact excited no interest at the time, but somebody later remembered it."

Bruce Milbank wondered at this odd beginning; the hikers also, he sensed, were curious as to what all this had to do with murder. Rogers asked Milbank for the first slide, and he flashed it on the screen. Odd, he thought. Why the fire lookout at Trumbull Peak? But Rogers was speaking.

"Buckingham before this time had taken a little vacation here in Yosemite. By the way, he was an eccentric sort. Did a little painting, and apparently when he moved about away from home he used an assumed name, the name in this instance being Wilsie. We get trace of Mr. Buckingham, alias Wilsie, at the fire lookout on Trumbull Peak last September. He signed the register there. And came on down into the Valley. Here I'm going to make an assumption. On that trip to Yosemite he ran across our erstwhile companion, Thomas Fulton, who, so Mr. Haverly tells me, as long ago as that was beginning to take long walks about the Valley floor to get himself in condition for the hike. The two struck up an acquaintance, but I'll come back to that later.

"Meantime," Rogers continued, as if he were launching upon a lecture in his class room, "we had Pearl Harbor, and the first weeks of confusion and alarms, and the first effort of the enemy here on the Pacific Coast to sink our shipping, and to shell the coast near Santa Barbara. It was odd that Mr. Buckingham chose this particular time to go out of the business of raising squabs.

"It is equally interesting that somebody remembered those squabs that were put aboard the departing Japanese liner. Somebody else in Contra Costa County thought it worth passing on that Mr. Buckingham had been interested in carrier pigeons as well as squabs. From that point it was only a step to another assumption that perhaps those squabs for which a liner would delay sailing ten minutes, as was the case, might have been carrier pigeons."

"Why!" A gasp of surprise escaped from Beryl Lindsay. "Have we had part in a plot?"

"If you choose to call it that," said Rogers evenly. He took up once more. "It was reasoned that whereas no carrier pigeon could fly from Japan to our West Coast, one could very easily fly to land from a submarine a few miles off shore. And if a pigeon did that, it would be for a particular purpose of getting word ashore about something of great importance to the enemy—and of vastly more concern to us.

"So a watch was set upon Buckingham's now empty pigeon loft. Buckingham, however, mysteriously had left for parts unknown. That was sometime last February. Incidentally, a pigeon did return to Buckingham's loft, and on its leg was a microfilm, which when 'blown up' to readable size disclosed some interesting information.

"I'll not go beyond this point. You're aware, of course, of the practicability of landing enemy agents from submarines in war time. Such persons require the aid of confederates on shore. The problem then becomes one not only of Mr. Buckingham, but of his associates as well. Who were they? Where were they? Buckingham had vanished. And with him all private papers, all data that might have furnished clues to his associates.

"Why does a man vanish before he has had an opportunity, say, to participate in the first venture of a well-planned plot? There are several answers. He might be done away with by his confederates for failure to play his part. It's not likely in this instance, however, because Buckingham already had performed a significant rôle. You can't change a carrier pigeon's homing instinct; you can't direct it to a new address, if in the meantime the family has moved. The proof that Buckingham had done his part is in the fact that the pigeons, several of them, at any rate, did return after Buckingham fled.

"Perhaps Buckingham got cold feet at the last minute and pulled out. That's another explanation. If Buckingham was associated in a ring to aid enemy agents, and he pulled out because he lacked courage to continue, then we might expect that he would be followed and killed, for the simple reason that he knew too much. This, as a matter of fact, is what happened."

Bruce Milbank felt Rogers' hand on his back, and he changed the picture on the screen. It was a scene along the trail. He thought he knew right where it was. Rogers went on.

"And here is a scene in Lost Valley where Buckingham's body was found ten days ago. It had lain in the snow since late last winter. Mr. Haverly was still endeavoring to identify the body at the time the hiking party was starting out last Monday morning. He succeeded in doing so only this morning when the dental work was traced through an Oakland dentist. Also, as you all know, Mr. Kramer last Monday when you went through Lost Valley found a hunting knife which very likely belonged to Buckingham."

The picture changed on the screen, and Rogers continued. "Here at Merced Lake camp occurred the murder of Mr. Hodges. The victim was an inoffensive gentleman known to Mr. Mullins from past association. There had been some trouble between them at one time. Conceivably it was of a character to furnish a motive for the killing. Further than that, Mr. Mullins visited the dead man's tent the morning of the discovery, and on his own word removed the knife from the dead man's body. The reason he gave was that he could not bear to see it in the body of his one-time friend.

"Now, that is a plausible action. But it raises the suspicion in the investigative mind: Was he the one to drive it into Hodges when the victim was still alive? Mr. Mullins, therefore, becomes a likely candidate for the murderer."

"Go on from there," came a voice in the semi-darkened room. It contained a note of warning.

"I'm going right on, Mr. Mullins," Rogers replied. "At this point it's necessary to remind you that Mr. Fulton changed tents with Mr. Hodges that evening about dinner time. Who knew of the change? Did Mr. Mullins know it? It's very doubtful. Miss Lindsay seems to have been the only one other than the two principals involved. So, if Mr. Mullins killed Hodges for the motive already given, how did he know where to find him in the dark? If Hodges, on the other hand, died because the murderer thought he was killing Mr. Fulton, then that changes the whole picture. Incidentally, the camp helper brought Mr. Dudley into the investigation by asserting that the knife was among Mr. Dudley's possessions in his tent, but whether the boy's imagination was at fault or not, I can't say. We couldn't find the knife. If the murderer decided to play a trick to throw suspicion upon someone else, he later changed his mind, for the knife didn't show up again until it was discovered to have been wished upon Mr. Turley."

"But tell us, Professor, who it is," Beryl Lindsay implored.

"I'll tell you soon enough."

25

BRUCE MILBANK felt a touch on his shoulder and changed the picture. The camp at Vogelsang stood out clearly. For a moment Rogers hesitated, then he went on again.

"The knife wasn't the only thing that was wished on somebody on this hike. Miss Benson at Merced Lake found a small piece of jade carved in the shape of a monkey among her things when she unrolled her pack. It wasn't hers; she'd never seen it before. And it was stolen from her at Vogelsang in the middle of the night. The thief returned with it to the dormitory tent and accidentally dropped it on the floor. His search was unavailing, because the jade monkey had dropped and bounced into Mr. Fulton's shoe. Fulton, incidentally, knew who this person was, as he intimated to Miss Benson. But apparently the significance of his knowledge did not make any impression upon him at the time. At any rate, he didn't act upon it as might be expected he would. He gave the piece of jade to Miss Benson next morning and asked her to keep it for him, and say nothing about it to anyone. Why? Miss Benson has no clear idea. Mr. Fulton, it seems, was beset with hunches about the piece of jade. It was not clear in his own mind what it was all about. The jade monkey had become important, but he didn't know why. And he took this means —giving it to Miss Benson—to preserve it. Apparently at no time, however, had it occurred to him that it was so important—that his own life depended upon it.

"After the party had left Vogelsang that morning, Mr.

Stoner went back to camp. Was it to look for the lost piece of jade, or a trout fly? He says it was the fly."

"And I still say it was the fly," said Stoner sharply, as if he felt himself being woven into the web.

Milbank flashed another picture on the screen. Rogers remarked casually. "These colored slides are beautiful things. The photographer who made them had the eye of an artist. You'll recognize the aspen forest at Glen Aulin. The deer on the trail is mere background. Mr. Fulton died here. Why? He was a wealthy man, and an old man. A lawyer who administers estates once remarked to me that wealthy persons who are old, like life tenants enjoying the income of trust funds, never seem to die. That is, to those who wait hopefully for the day of inheritance.

"Curiously, although plausibly, as you all know from what transpired after the death of Mr. Fulton, we have a niece and her husband—kept under wraps, so to speak, until it was all over—and a daughter and her husband in the party. Ample motive, ample opportunity. If Mr. Mullins at Merced Lake killed Hodges by mistake, thinking he was killing Mr. Fulton, from whom his wife would inherit considerable money, did he eventually succeed at Glen Aulin? Did Mr. DeWitt commit the crime—possibly, also, being guilty of Hodges' death?"

"I did not!" exclaimed DeWitt. "Don't start that again!"

"That's what you say, Al," came the raucous voice of Hammond.

"Never mind," DeWitt retorted menacingly.

"It becomes quite a problem, doesn't it?" said Rogers as if he was interested in this outbreak. "You might think that in investigating this series of crimes, Mr. Plummer at this point would be justified in making an arrest. A really strong case, although circumstantial, could be made against either Mr. DeWitt or Mr. Mullins. Especially the latter. Mr. Stoner apparently is a weak runner-up. There's no motive in his case. I don't see, so far as has been developed in our discussion, that Mr. Dudley figures very strongly, either, in these two crimes. But if there's another motive behind the two crimes, what then?"

Milbank felt a touch on his shoulder once more and he changed the slides. He recognized the place on the trail as it crossed the high ridges between Glen Aulin and May Lake. In the background was Mount Hoffman.

"The pattern to this point is a fairly obvious one. The Hodges death could be an accident killing; he was in the wrong tent. Mr. Fulton died because he had much money —and impatient heirs. It's happened, I regret to remind you, thousands of times in the history of the world.

"But—" Rogers' tone was sharp, "if this is so, how explain what happened to Miss Benson yesterday afternoon on the trail here? What did she know about the two crimes that would endanger her life? This is where the pattern changes, and we have to look about for a different explanation, or a different motive. Up to this point Miss Benson had carried on her person the small piece of jade carved in the shape of a monkey. Unknown to anyone else in the party, now that Mr. Fulton was dead. Unless, of course, it figured in what had already happened. In which case the person who stole the jade monkey at Vogelsang, only to lose it, was still in the party and still bent on obtaining it, even at the cost of another life. In which case, could we not assume that Mr. Fulton had died not because he was a wealthy man with impatient heirs, but rather because he was suspected of having the piece of jade on his person? Or did the murderer possibly suspect that Mr. Fulton knew who he was, after what happened at Vogelsang? Miss Benson has told me that Mr. Fulton intimated that he knew the man's identity. Still another consideration, at the time of his death had Mr. Fulton been forced to disclose the whereabouts of the bit of jade? Or did the murderer reason that Claudia Benson had it once more in her possession?"

Al DeWitt broke in upon Rogers. "Oh, oh! Jack," he said, "here's where you get yours. Will you give me your autograph before you go to the gas chamber?"

"I didn't," said Hammond in a sort of croak. "All I know is I found it underneath her when I tried to pick her up. How do I know anything about it? It was a piece of green rock shaped like a monkey. I was going to give it back to her—"

"But nobody would have known you had it," protested Beryl Lindsay accusingly, "if I hadn't accidentally turned my flashlight on you last night and saw it in your hand."

"That ain't so!" said Hammond. "I was going to give it back."

"It's just possible," Rogers interrupted, "that Mr. Fulton would be alive today if, instead of giving the thing to Miss Benson and requesting that she keep silent about it, he had given it to Bruce Milbank with an explanation of how he got it. Whether or not he knew its significance there is now no way of knowing for certain. I rather think he suspected its nature—I must assume it—or he would not have tried to make Miss Benson its sanctuary. But mistakes like that can't be altered.

"I'm going back to Buckingham, if you don't mind,"

Rogers said after a short pause. "I said at the outset that when he decamped from his pigeon loft it might have been because he had got cold feet. But could it be possible that there was another reason? Did he see the possibility of blackmail? Buckingham was an intelligent fellow. He expected, of course, that his action would bring down the vengeance of his associates. He expected to be followed. The fact that he took refuge in the Ahwahnee hotel makes it quite plain, I think, that he expected to be followed. For a man in his modest circumstances wouldn't choose that particular place to hole up; it is the last place he would be expected to go, I imagine.

"But having met Mr. Fulton the previous summer, as I have assumed, he thought of it as a place in which to hide temporarily from his pursuers. Did he mature his blackmail plot at the hotel, and then get in touch with one of his associates? There was evidence that he had thought out at least the preliminary part of his scheme before he came up to Yosemite, evidence that he had made use of certain documents and then burned them in the fireplace where he lived.

"None of you hikers know why Mr. Plummer and I came down to the Valley floor from Tuolumne Meadows. It was to discover, if possible, what occurred at the hotel where Mr. Fulton and Buckingham lived during a critical period last winter. It was at this time that Mr. Fulton acquired the jade monkey. As a gift from Buckingham. At any time, of course, during these weeks, Buckingham, if he had been inclined to do so, could have got in touch with the federal authorities and given them the information he had. But he did not do so, which is further proof that he planned blackmail, or was holding out for a price.

"This leads to an assumption at this point. Buckingham got in touch with his confederates, or one of them of his choosing. And this person came to Yosemite. They began negotiating for the information Buckingham had to sell back to the ring. But it ended in failure. Although Buckingham had something readily saleable, what guaranty could he give that he would not also talk? Because he had not solved that point is why he came to grief. Buckingham became frightened. He saw that his game was up. He had given Mr. Fulton the jade monkey. He fled now in panic from the hotel. There was heavy snow on the ground, but he started on snowshoes up the trail from Happy Isles. Probably he had a wild notion that he could escape by way of Tioga Pass, for he had inquired at the fire lookout on Trumbull Peak the summer before when the pass would be snowed in. The facts are indicative not only of his panic but of his long scheming. He was overtaken in Lost Valley and killed.

"Now, then, what happened there in the snow before he died? Was he forced to tell where he had hidden the evidence that would disclose the plot? Or did he boast of it, like a man taunting his murderer when death is imminent with information that in his safe deposit box would be found the name of his slayer? Or did the killer, after the crime was committed, search the body—as he undoubtedly did—and not finding what he looked for, sit down later and by cold analysis figure out in what form and where he was to find it? I think he did the latter. Because he is a shrewd man.

"Mr. Fulton's room was searched that morning after he had left to join the party at Happy Isles. Mr. and Mrs. DeWitt, you visited the hotel that morning, seeking Mr.

Fulton. You were uncertain—"

"I told you we didn't go up to his room at all," shouted DeWitt. "We didn't."

A raucous laugh came from Jack Hammond. Then silence followed. Rogers took up where he had left off. "I wonder if Mr. Fulton ever realized that he was being stalked. And yet toward the last he must have. There was a telephone call vaguely threatening; there was a mysterious note which unfortunately he destroyed. Months of scheming, of watching and waiting must have gone into the murderer's effort to discover where and in what form this deadly information was preserved. Very likely he never let Mr. Fulton out of his sight toward the end. He ransacked Mr. Fulton's room that morning and then not discovering what he was seeking joined the hiking party for which he'd already made a reservation in case Mr. Fulton carried the jade monkey with him.

"You may have wondered what sort of evidence Buckingham had to sell. In what form was it? And why the jade monkey? You're familiar, of course, with microfilm. The pictures in these slides you've been looking at are a kind of microfilm."

Milbank felt a touch on his shoulder and he switched the slides. Instead of the usual picture of Yosemite scenery a typewritten document flashed on the screen. In it there was a short column of names and addresses.

"This is what I have reference to," said Rogers. "Buckingham photographed all the information he had about the activities of the ring. There's more than what you see here, by the way. And in a few moments I'll show you how by twisting the jade monkey's head to one side it comes out like the stopper in a bottle, and in the little space inside there's room for a fairsized book in microfilm—"

"Oh, there's Bill Turley's name!" exclaimed Beryl Lindsay in shocked amazement. "Right there among the others. Why! Bill—"

"Turley!" exclaimed Doug Kramer. "Turley's—"

"Bill! Bill! Wake up!" said Beryl Lindsay curiously, shaking him by the shoulder.

The lights flashed on, and Plummer jerked open the blind at a window. The figure beside the school teacher did not rouse. Slowly, like a drunken man, it reeled from its chair and fell upon the floor.

"He's dead! He's killed himself," said Miss Lindsay in a strange voice. "Oh, I can smell the cyanide now."

"He thought of everything, didn't he?" said Plummer grimly as he stood over him.

The last good-byes were spoken, the last handshakes exchanged, and the door closed upon the final hiker. Milbank picked up his hat.

"Don't hurry, Bruce," said Superintendent Haverly. "Sit down."

"I was just wondering," said the assistant park naturalist. "I don't remember a single name on that list myself, except Turley's. You don't suppose, though, that anybody else in the crowd would remember those names and the information get out before something could be done about arresting the others in the ring. Not that the hikers would deliberately—"

Plummer laughed. "The professor thinks of everything too, Bruce."

The superintendent was smiling. "What you saw, Bruce, was a dummy list, except for Turley's name. Even I couldn't tell you who else is involved. Those persons already are being rounded up. Professor Rogers, you know, has had several hours in which to work. The little show was fixed up for the benefit of your party."

Plummer turned to Rogers, who sat back in his chair with his eyes closed. "When did you first suspect Turley, Hunt?"

"Much too late, Floyd. If I had known earlier that Turley had been stopping for several weeks at the Ahwahnee I might have thought of him in connection with the ransacking of Mr. Fulton's room. But I didn't learn that until just before we left May Lake last night to take Mr. Haverly and the doctor down to the Tioga Road. He must have been there in the hotel, watching and plotting how to get his hands upon the information that Buckingham had left with the old man in the jade monkey. He was taking no chances, for he planned to go on the hike with Mr. Fulton. The chance to get into the old man's room must have come suddenly that morning after Mr. Fulton left."

"He was late in arriving at Happy Isles," said Milbank. "The last one, in fact. Funny how I missed so many clues myself."

"When the knife fell out of his pack yesterday on the trail, though, I began to wonder," Rogers took up. "Doug Kramer was quick to exonerate Turley then. But a knife is easily concealed about the person. Turley's play was for sympathy. Like Dudley, he wanted to be thought an innocent victim of the murderer. Incidentally, he must have planted the knife in Dudley's tent at Merced Lake and, after the boy there had seen it, taken it away again. If

Dudley had been the murderer, he'd never have left the knife where it could be plainly seen. Turley was clever, far more clever than the average murderer, and this was a sort of flourish to call attention to his cleverness.

"But if you'll think back to Claudia Benson for a moment, just before she was nearly killed on the trail. She'd been talking with Turley. Miss Forbes dropped back and Turley went on ahead. When Claudia left Miss Forbes behind her, she next encountered Mullins. Immediately after running on ahead of him, the murderer made his attack upon her. But when the positions of the various hikers on the trail were made known later, we find Turley coming up with Dudley, who was behind Mullins and Miss Forbes. Where, therefore, had Turley been, and how had he managed to alter his position on the trail without anybody seeing him? Hadn't he been the one to waylay Claudia? Didn't he then backtrack off the trail and join Dudley?"

"After that, then," remarked Haverly, "Turley was the man to watch?"

"Yes."

"But how did he miss finding the jade monkey?" asked Plummer. "That's what he was after, and why he nearly killed the girl."

"There's a simple explanation, I believe," said Rogers. "Claudia told us that the last thing she remembered was walking with her hands in her pockets, holding the jade monkey in her left hand. So, when the blow was struck, her hands must have come suddenly out of her pockets and with them the monkey, which dropped out of her hand when she relaxed and she either fell or rolled upon the piece of jade. Hammond, I concluded, was right when he said that he found it underneath her when he started to pick her up. Turley couldn't have had much time in which to work. Only a hurried search was possible before he heard Hammond coming."

Plummer heaved a sigh of deep relief. "I'm glad it's all over, Boss. But we certainly draw some queer ones to Yosemite."

"Meaning whom, Floyd?"

"Miss Forbes. Why in the world would she tell the story she told about her husband and his adventures in South America?"

"Throwing her husband to the lions, as it were," laughed Rogers. "She could have kept still about the whole thing. It didn't mean anything in the final analysis."

"She was a peculiar woman. Maybe she was hoping to get rid of Mullins so she could marry again. At any rate, if all his family were like her, you couldn't blame poor old Mr. Fulton for coming to Yosemite to retire."

A knock sounded on the door, and Milbank got up at the superintendent's nod to open it. Douglas Kramer stood in the doorway, and behind him was Claudia Benson. Kramer suddenly held out his hand to Milbank.

"Sorry to interrupt," he said. "I just wanted to thank you again, ranger." He seemed slightly embarrassed. "At Happy Isles that morning Claudia would have pulled out of the party if it hadn't been for you. She just said so. And—well—could you get off to come down to a wedding next week?"

"Why—probably—I'll—"

"Of course you can, Bruce," said Haverly. "And—if Miss Benson—"

Claudia Benson pushed her way into the room past Doug Kramer. Her tanned cheeks were flushed and her eyes sparkled.

"Would you come, really—all of you?"

"Yes." The answer came as a chorus.